by Rachel Gibson

I Do!

By Rachel Gibson

I Do!

RACHEL GIBSON

AVONIMPULSE

An Imprint of HarperCollinsPublishers

An excerpt from *What I Love About You* copyright © 2014 by Rachel Gibson.

EPub Edition JANUARY 2015 ISBN: 9780062247513
Print Edition ISBN: 9780062247520

10 9 8 7 6 5 4 3 2 1

I Do!

Chapter 1

AT THE AGE of twenty-three, Rebecca Ramsey had found her passion. Her love. Her creative calling. While some artists worked in oil or fabrics or clay, Becca worked in hair. While other girls her age were still in college trying to figure out what to do with their lives, Becca had mapped hers all out. Since graduating from the Milan (Texas, not Italy) Institute of Cosmetology a few years ago, she'd worked diligently perfecting her passion. Her love. Her art. Becca was good at cuts and blowouts, fabulous with highlights, ombres, peekaboos, and dip-dyes, but when it came to the updo, she was a true master. She excelled at creating everything from simple French knots to complicated runway hair, complete with twigs and birds and working fountains.

Of course, there wasn't a lot of demand for runway hair in Amarillo, Texas, where she lived and worked, and absolutely none at all sixty miles north in the small town of Lovett where she'd been born and raised. But this *was* Texas, where special occasion hair was in high demand. "The bigger the hair the closer to God" was not just a saying in the northern panhandle, it was like the eleventh commandment: Thou shalt have big hair.

Proms, graduations, and Becca's favorite, bridal hair, kept her elbow-deep in complicated chignons and styling product. She loved big occasions that called for big hair and had big plans to open her own salon in the future. She hadn't quite settled on a name, but she had some time yet to think about it. She figured she could call it something catchy like Becca's Bangz and Beauty, or Becca's Flair for Hair. Or she could go for classy, like Salon B or Creative Hair Design. Or she could go for fun and funky like Fringe or Bouffant.

Beneath the bright June sun, Becca reached across the seat of her Volkswagen Beetle and grabbed her sunglasses out of her Coach bag sitting on top of several bridal magazines. She slid on her cat-eye sunglasses like she was Audrey Hepburn and adjusted the visor. Typical of a Sunday afternoon in the panhandle, traffic from Amarillo to Lovett was sparse except for the occasional truck pulling a bass fishing boat or a couple of four-wheelers.

Becca had driven this particular stretch of road so many times, she drove by rote, barely noticing the clumps of grasses and windmills stirred by the breeze. Her right front tire hit a dead armadillo as she recalled the salon name she'd thought up right before she'd fallen asleep the night before. Sometimes, her best inspiration happened just before sleep, like the Retro Cinderella or

Crystal Chandelier updos she'd envisioned and then perfected for her portfolio.

Last night she'd thought Head House had seemed like a great name for a salon, but now in light of day and a clearer mind, it sounded more like a bordello.

Becca slowed and took the off ramp for Lovett. Just last week, local photographer Daisy Parrish had come into Lily Belle's Salon and Day Spa where Becca worked to take photographs of Becca's latest inspired wedding hairstyles. Because Daisy and the owner of the spa, Lily, were sisters, Daisy gave a big discount to everyone who worked at the salon. Both sisters were beautiful and talented in their own ways, Daisy with her camera and Lily with the spa. They were so classy and seemed so happy that it was hard to believe the old gossip about the two brawling at the Gas and Go years ago.

Becca didn't have time for gossip and was much too busy to care about a beat-down over Lily's cheating exhusband and his slutty girlfriend at a convenience store. All that had happened when Becca was in middle school. She hadn't heard any gossip about the sisters lately. Then again, she'd lived in Amarillo for a year now and didn't hear hometown gossip every time she stopped to fill her car with gas or grabbed some breakfast at the Wild Coyote. She didn't hear much at all unless her mother called to fill her in. Which was quite often, actually.

Right now, talk in Lovett revolved around the wedding of Sadie Hollowell and Vince Haven. It seemed the small town had its collective panties in a bunch because the couple had chosen to have the wedding at the JH

Ranch—named after Sadie's late father, Clive Hollowell—with only close friends and relatives in attendance.

There were a lot of people in town who thought Sadie owed them a "big doin's" simply because the Hollowells had settled in the panhandle when Lovett had been nothing more than a stage stop and general store. The ranch was a deeply imbedded part of Texas history. Almost as much as the Alamo to the South, but without the revolution or siege or James Bowie.

Secretly, Becca wished the wedding was going to be a "big doin's," too. Not because she thought Sadie owed her anything, but she was styling the bridal hair. A big wedding would have been a great way for people to see her work.

Becca stopped at a red light in the middle of town and touched up her pink lip gloss. After one quick stop to fetch the latest photos Daisy had left for her, Becca was heading to the JH and a final meeting with Sadie before the ceremony next Saturday.

Sadie was more than Becca's latest bride client. She was engaged to Becca's good friend Vince Haven, and had become Becca's friend, too. So much so that Sadie had not only hired Becca to do her wedding hair, she'd included Becca in some of the planning. She'd sought her advice on flowers and the arbor and the maid of honor dress.

Vince had been no help at all. His favorite colors were brown and dark brown, and talk of flowers made him fold his arms over his big chest and scowl. Sadie's sister, Stella, wasn't much help, either. Stella was busy with her own life and own fiancé, and frankly, Stella wasn't a Texan. Like Vince, she didn't understand that a simple wedding was never simple, and Stella's tastes ran more toward leather and combat boots than toward lace and satin pumps.

Bless her heart.

The light turned green and Becca took off. She changed lanes in front of an old pickup truck that moved too slow. She didn't have time for slow. She had a client list to build, money to make, and a bride waiting to see the latest updo photos Daisy had taken for her portfolio.

It was a good thing Sadie had enlisted Becca's help, because even though Becca would never say it out loud, Sadie wasn't very good at special occasion planning, and neither was the local event planner she'd hired. Vince's sister, Autumn, was a wedding planner, but Autumn lived in Seattle and could do little but offer advice from seventeen hundred miles away.

Becca slowed and turned her car into Parrish American Classics. The auto restoration business was closed and she pulled the Beetle in a slot near the front doors. Daisy and her family were boating at Lake Meredith for the weekend, but Daisy had volunteered to leave the portfolio in the mailbox at her husband's business.

The afternoon sun glinted off the lenses of Becca's sunglasses as she got out of the car and spotted the big mailbox nailed near the front doors. Most of the wedding guests were Sadie's relatives and Vince's military buddies. Becca had briefly met two of those buddies, twin brothers Blake and Beau Junger. The brothers were big and kind of scary and so identical it was freaky.

The sounds of vehicles passing on the street, and the distant stream of hard rock music, filled Becca's ears as stuck her hand inside mailbox. She didn't feel anything and rose onto the toes of her T-strap wedges and looked inside. It was empty.

So she tried the front doors of the business. They rattled but didn't open. She knocked and yelled hello a few times, then followed the sound of the heavy metal music around the side of the building. The wooden heels of her crocheted sandals tapped across the concrete. She'd paid seventy bucks for the shoes, a big splurge for a girl on a tight budget, but she just hadn't been able to resist the color: Scarlet Tango.

Her last boyfriend liked to say that women who wore red didn't wear panties, but Toby Ray had said a lot of things like they were facts instead of something he'd made up in his own dumb head. No one had ever confused Toby Ray for a deep thinker, but then again, no girl dated that boy for his mind.

Bless his heart.

Becca's shadow followed her as she rounded the building, and the warm June breeze ruffled the bottom of her white and red sundress. The slight wind tossed a few strands of her medium blond hair, brightened with perfectly placed level nine highlights. The heavy drumbeat and screeching vocals assaulted her ears, and from behind the lenses of her sunglasses, her gaze landed on a gleaming red convertible parked at an angle behind the garage. Tiny bursts of sunlight glistened in the cherry-colored paint, dancing along the front fenders to the tip of the pointed fins in back. The raised hood had a Cadillac emblem. This was Texas, where trucks and Cadillacs ruled, but other than a limo, or maybe the stretch hearse from Alden Funeral and Crematorium, it was the longest car Becca had ever seen. Some people might look at it and see a classic. Becca saw a pimp mobile, and if there was one car in which she never wanted to be seen, it was a shiny pimp mobile with tuck and roll leather seats.

A Beats speaker and an iPod rested on the ground by the front whitewall tire, and a pair of legs from the thighs down stuck out from beneath the chrome bumper and massive grille. Presumably the legs belonged to a male. A male wearing faded jeans on his legs and gray Vans on his feet. In Lovett, Texas, men wore Justin Boots. Not skater shoes. It was kind of startling. Like if someone stuck a Prius at Cadillac Ranch.

She glanced around, then continued past the long car and the skater shoes and toward the two-story house several hundred feet behind the garage. The house looked newly painted, white with green trim and yellow window boxes. The window boxes were empty and the front door was open.

Becca knocked on the screen door several times, but like the front of the business, no one answered. She peered through the screen and into the dark interior and at the outline of a sofa, a comfy-looking recliner, and a big-screen television. "Is anyone home?" When she still got no answer, she retraced her steps to the front fender of the Cadillac.

"Hello," she called out over the horrible music.

Instead of an answer, a deep male voice rose from beneath the car and sang along with the music, if it could be called music. It was more a pounding assault of guitars and drums and motherfuck this and motherfuck that. The voice beneath the car was worse than the lead singer/screecher, which Becca would have thought impossible. She unplugged the iPod, then leaned under the raised hood. She cupped her hands around her mouth and yelled, "Hello!"

A hollow thud like someone thumped a watermelon came from beneath the car. A loud "Shit" mingled with the sound of tools hitting concrete.

Becca wrinkled her nose and whispered, "Ouch." She straightened to the sound of a painful moan and a few "goddamn its." Then two greasy hands reached from beneath and grabbed the shiny bumper. Under the smudges of grease, the head of a Chinese dragon breathed fire across the back of his hand. Squeaky little wheels rolled the rest of him from under the car. Long legs and a spiky belt led to a dirt-smudged white T-shirt over a flat belly. Next came hard forearms and balls of muscular shoulders. The rest of the dragon tattoo wrapped up his arm, and the tail disappeared under the T-shirt sleeve. His square chin and jaw were covered in dark stubble, and a frown pulled at the corners of his mouth. Then eyes the color of a clear Texas sky slid into view and stared up at her. Angry blue eyes beneath dark slashes of brows and surrounded by dark lashes. An even angrier red mark on his forehead seemed to turn redder by the second.

Despite the furious scowl and horrible welt, hideous

spiky belt and tacky tattoo, he was so ridiculously hot, Becca felt her insides melt. "You're not at the lake," she managed past her suddenly dry throat.

"Obviously." He rubbed a greasy hand across the welt on his forehead. "Can I do something for you?"

"Yes." She'd met guys like him before. Guys who looked good in anything from tight T-shirts and jeans to a Sunday suit and tie. Guys who looked at a girl and took her breath away. She'd always been a sucker for guys like him. Hot guys with cool names like Tucker or Slade or Toby Ray. Or, in this case, Nathan Parrish.

"Are you going to share with the rest of the class?"

"What?" She'd never *personally* met Nate. He'd graduated high school three years before her, but she didn't have to know him personally to know his personal history. Everyone in Lovett knew it.

"What do you need?" He sat up and she took a step back.

Oh! "Photographs. I'm supposed to pick up my photographs."

He rose to his feet and pulled a dirty blue shop towel from the back pocket of his jeans. "My mother isn't here," he said as he wiped his hands.

Even in her heels, he was a good head taller than she, and she took another step back. He smelled like oil and sweat. She should be repulsed. "I know. She said she'd leave them in the mailbox." Yeah, she should be repulsed, but she'd always been a sucker for guys like him. Good-looking guys who were good with their hands. Guys who borrowed money from nice girls like her for gas or rent or food. Or to take tramps like Lexie Jane Johnson to Rowdy's Roadhouse for twofer night.

He wiped the web between his long fingers as a clear bead of sweat slid from his scruffy jaw and down his neck. "Did you check the box before you walked back here and ripped the cord out of my iPod?"

"Yes I checked." His hair was so dark and thick that one bead of sweat probably contained enough intoxicating pheromones to turn the heads of every female from Dalhart to Abilene. "And I didn't rip anything. I unplugged it." After her last breakup, she'd sworn off hot guys with hot toxic pheromones. "Sorry I scared you."

He slowly lifted his gaze up her chest and throat to her mouth. His eyes, a cool, clear blue surrounded by those black lashes, looked into hers and sent tingles to the backs of her knees. "I wasn't scared. Girls in big red shoes and Texas hair don't scare me." He tossed the towel on the car's engine. "I was startled. There's a difference."

Big shoes! Her feet were only a six and a half. "If you say so."

"You nearly gave me a concussion."

The old Becca would have felt bad and been totally susceptible to his hot eyes giving her warm tingles. The old Becca would have succumbed to his lethal good looks and said something flirty. The new Becca ignored her tingles and her urge to feel bad for causing the welt on his head. "Sorry I startled you, and you nearly gave yourself a concussion." She was so pleased that she hadn't so much as flipped her "Texas hair" that she added, "Although, if that crappy music you listen to doesn't give you brain damage, nothing will."

A scowl creased his forehead right beneath the red bump getting redder. "Says the girl who probably listens to Taylor Swift."

"What's wrong with Taylor Swift?" She liked Taylor Swift. Nothing better after a bad breakup than a bag of Hershey's Kisses, a box of Kleenex, and "Picture to Burn" downloaded onto her phone.

"Shitty chick music." He moved toward the house and added over his shoulder as he walked up the steps, "And that's the best thing that can be said about Taylor Swift."

That was three insults in less than a minute, her feet, her hair, and her taste in music. Becca's gaze slid from the back of his dark head, past the comma of curls at the base of his neck, to the shoulders of his T-shirt covered in grime. The screen door hinges squeaked and her gaze slipped down his back to his waist and that stupid spiky belt. What a jerk.

"Your photos are probably in the house." He paused halfway inside and glanced over his shoulder at her. "Come in out of the heat while I look for them." The darker shadows of the porch hid the top of his face and slashed across his nose to the corner of his mouth and the dark stubble on his chin.

Go inside Nathan Parrish's house? She didn't think he was a demented pervert. At least she hadn't heard anything about him being a demented pervert. But she didn't know him, and it wasn't smart for a girl to go into the house of a man she didn't know. "I'll wait here."

"Suit yourself." He shrugged.

The screen door slapped shut behind him and Becca tried to recall what she did know of Nate. She let out a puff of breath as she dug back into her memory. She hadn't heard much about him for a while now. Not since the big scandal involving him and Lindsey Dale when Lindsey had gone around town telling everyone that one night of passionate love with Nate had created a love child. The town had fed on that gossip for seven months until it became obvious to everyone that Nate was not the father. The dates just hadn't matched, neither had the DNA test Nate demanded on Lindsey's baby girl.

For one whole summer people whispered and wondered about that baby's daddy. There had been a ton of speculation, but no real confirmation until the day Bug Larson's wife had chased him through a field down by the high school, swearing "You cheating son of a bitch" at the top of her lungs and swinging a baseball bat.

Becca shook her head. Sometimes Lovett, Texas, was as scandalous as the *Maury Show*. Not that she watched.

A frown creased her brow above the frame of her sunglasses. When had that been the hottest event in town? Three years ago maybe? She knew it had been right after she'd graduated beauty school and landed her first job at Karla's Kuts and Kurls. She'd spent that summer squandering her versatile talents with cut and color on the shampoo-and-set ladies for minimum wage and dollar tips. All they'd talked about was Nathan Parrish and Lindsey Dale and how they weren't the least surprised, given that Nate's parents had created enough of their own scandals and how Lindsey was just the last in a long line of Dale loose women.

She looked at her watch. After the baseball bat incident, Lindsey's mom had packed up her and her baby and sent them off to her cousin in Huntsville, which just seemed like cruel and unusual punishment, as far was Becca was concerned. She remembered hearing that Nate had returned to college up north somewhere, but she hadn't heard much about him after that.

Of course, she'd moved and didn't pay attention to gossip.

Her hand fell to the side and her gaze returned to the front door. If Nate didn't hurry, she was going to be late for her meeting with Sadie. What was taking him so long? Had he fallen and hit his head again? She was baking beneath the Texas sun. The top of her head was getting cooked and it was apparent that he was in no hurry to reappear and didn't care if she died of heatstroke.

Bless his pea-pickin' heart.

The heels of her shoes tapped on the concrete as she walked up the steps and across the wooden porch. While it might not be smart to go into a man's house alone, time was money, and he was wasting hers. Instead of knocking again, or calling out, she slowly opened the front screen door.

A BROAD SLICE of sunlight slipped between toile curtains, bleached with age, and spilled across Nate's bare shoulders and chest. He scrubbed his face with a clean washcloth, thick with suds from a bar of Irish Spring. He stood in his work pants at the chipped single-basin sink, his shoes planted in the spot worn thin by generations of Parrish men washing up after work. Cold water from the faucet streamed full force into the sink and splashed droplets on his belly and the thin line of dark hair that circled his navel and disappeared beneath the waistband riding low on his hips.

Nate had lived alone in this house, his grandparents' house, since the day he'd moved back to Lovett full-time to work with his father and Uncle Billy at Parrish American Classics a little over a year ago.

Suds dripped from his chin as he slid the washrag to the back of his neck and across his shoulders. For the first fifteen years of his life, he'd lived in Seattle. He'd been born and raised there by his mother and stepfather, Steven Monroe. After his stepfather's death, his mother had moved them back to Texas so he could get to know his biological father, Jack Parrish. He and his dad had adjusted to each other easily, but he'd never quite adjusted to Lovett. Not the small town. Not the gossip. Not the dry heat.

He rinsed the cloth beneath the cold tap water. When it had come time to choose a college after graduating from high school, he'd naturally chosen the University of Washington. He'd lived in Seattle for six years, returning to Texas on holidays and in the summer to see his family. He loved Seattle, but Nate discovered he was a Parrish like his dad and uncle. Oil ran through their veins and he loved the smell of 15W–50. There was nothing like a fully restored American beauty. Nothing turned Nate on more than a 427 big block vibrating the pavement. Nothing like four-barrel carbs, flat open and chewing up the road, to make him hard.

Soap stung a cut under his chin and he leaned at the waist and stuck his head beneath the faucet. Cold water ran over his head and down his cheeks. The '66 Cadillac in the driveway made him hard. Real hard, and if Holly Ann wasn't in Dallas for the summer, he wouldn't mind tossing her on the Coupe Deville's big trunk and testing out the suspension. He'd set her between the glossy red fins and step between her open thighs. She'd tilt her face to his and he'd kiss her mouth as he had sex with his girlfriend of one year.

The chilly water on the back of his neck felt good after working under Cadillac, and he paused to let it run through his hair and down his temples and the welt on his forehead. Of course, Holly Ann probably wouldn't go for it. She didn't like grease and dirt and outdoor sex.

The girl in the white dress in his driveway probably wasn't the kind of girl who'd go for it, either. Not that he was interested, but she looked like one of those good girls. The kind that didn't like to get messed up. The kind who teased guys with red polish on her toenails and red shoes that made her legs incredibly long. The kind who wore a white dress that the sun shone through and outlined her inner thighs clear up to the V of her crotch. Between the sunlight and those big sunglasses, he hadn't seen much of her face. Her legs were memorable, though.

He felt around for the cold tap and turned it off. She

was probably melting out there, but it wasn't his fault. He'd told her to come inside. He was sweaty and grimy and needed to clean up before he looked for his mother's photos. She'd worked hard to establish her name, and the last thing she needed was a set of black fingerprints on the white studio folder. And since he was washing his hands, he figured he'd wash the rest of him, too.

He ran his hands over the back of his head and down his face. It was probably best the girl stayed outside anyway. Holly Ann wouldn't appreciate it if he invited a girl into his house, and while he'd begun to question his relationship with her, he had to respect the year they'd been together.

Nate blew the water from his lips and straightened. He shook his head like a dog and sent droplets across the kitchen and down his back. There had been a time in his life when he would have already stepped out on Holly Ann, but Nate was not a cheater. Not these days. He'd learned a long time ago that one-night stands with girls he didn't know were never worth it.

A fluffy blue bath towel sat on the counter next to a clean T-shirt. He reached for the towel and covered his head with it. He scrubbed it over his hair and dried his face. He hadn't hooked up with a nameless girl for several years now. Not since Lindsey Dale had accused him of being her baby's daddy. Not since the night his father had called him to ask about the story she'd been spreading around town. Not since the night he'd had to tell his dad that he didn't remember her name or face, but he did remember meeting her at Rowdy's Roadhouse when he'd been home for Christmas. He remembered her sticking her hand down his pants and having sex with her in the backseat of his '67 Camaro. He'd been shit-faced, but he'd remembered to use a condom.

He scrubbed the towel across his back and neck, then slipped it over the top of his head once more. No one in town had believed him about the condom. No one but his family, and while they had all supported and believed him, that whole summer had been difficult on everyone. Especially his parents. It had brought back painful memories for them. Memories of a past they didn't talk about because it had been resolved. Memories that had the potential to hurt, and it did no one any good to pick at a sore spot.

The towel fell to his shoulders and everything in him stilled. He heard a faint intake of breath and spun around at the sound. The girl from the driveway stood in the entrance to the kitchen; light poured into the living room and backlit her once again like an angel come down from heaven. An angel with sunbeams in her golden hair and sliding over her bare shoulders to dip into her smooth cleavage. His own breath whooshed from his lungs as if a hard fist slammed into his chest.

"I didn't want to call out and scare you again," she said, and pushed her sunglasses to the top of her head.

Sweet Lord Jesus, other than his mom coming over to do his laundry, he hadn't had a female in his house for so long he'd forgotten how they changed the air in a room. "Startle." He tossed the towel on the counter and grabbed his shirt. He'd forgotten how a woman could turn the air instantly hot.

"Potato, pa-tot-o."

She was a smartass. A good girl smartass. He shoved his arms into the sleeves of the armadillo T-shirt his twelve-year-old cousin had given to him last Christmas, then pulled it over his head. She looked like a good girl. A good girl who made him have very bad thoughts. Thoughts of a certain Northern boy kissing her pink lips, then sliding his mouth south to her Dixieland. He wasn't surprised by his thoughts. He'd always had a taste for good girls.

"How's your head?"

He'd forgotten about it and raised his hand to the welt. He pressed it with his fingertips and winced. "Hurts like a bitch."

"Sorry." Her little smile twisted her pink lips, and she didn't look sorry at all. She moved farther into the kitchen, and with each step of her red shoes, his chest got a little tighter. One step and then two and the tight feeling in his chest slid down his insides to grip him beneath his belt. Three steps, then four, and his ball sac got tight and reminded him just how long Holly Ann had been away. She stopped in front of him and stuck out her hand. "I'm Becca Ramsey. I work for your aunt Lily."

Nate looked down into her face tilted up a few inches beneath his. Her eyes were the brilliant blue of morning glories that grew along his grandmother's fence. "Let me guess." He took her hand, and the warmth of her palm seeped into his. "You wax eyebrows and armpits."

"I cut, style, and color hair. Sorry if you were looking for someone to get rid of that uni-brow for you." She laughed at her little joke like she was amusing, but he didn't have a uni-brow and she wasn't funny. Somehow, none of that mattered as the soft sound of laughter whispered across his skin and sent a shiver up his spine. "Are you cold?"

Holy shit. He pulled his hand from hers and away from her touch. Hell no, he wasn't cold. He was hot. Hot for a girl in a white dress and red shoes. He swallowed past the sudden constriction in his throat and wondered for half a second if he'd accidentally gotten ahold of some shellfish. Shellfish made his mouth itch and his throat close. Earlier he'd eaten a huge bowl of Cocoa Puffs. That was it.

She looked up at him through those shiny blue eyes and her smile fell. "Are you okay?"

Hell no, he wasn't okay. His chest felt tight, like he was having an allergic reaction when he hadn't eaten anything he was allergic to. He had a painful case of hard dick for a girl who wasn't his girlfriend.

"Can I get ice for your head?"

She put a concerned hand on his forearm, and he lowered his gaze to her thin fingers and red nails. The feeling in his chest and belly had nothing to do with shellfish and everything to do with this girl. "No." His brow lowered and reminded him that he'd whacked his head pretty good. Maybe he'd knocked his head harder than he'd thought. Maybe his reaction was some sort of concussion. A delayed concussion that tightened his insides and made every hair on his body rise like he was standing in a freezer. "But you need to go," he said before he tried to make her stay. "Now." He shook off her touch and walked through the kitchen to the living room.

"My photographs," she reminded him as she trailed behind. "I need my photographs."

Her opened the door and held it for her. "I looked," he lied. "My mom must have forgotten to drop them off."

She stopped on the porch and turned to gaze up at him. "I just spoke to her yesterday." The corners of her brows lowered as if he was crazy. "She said she left them in the mailbox."

He felt crazy. "She must have lied." He'd just called his mother a liar. Now he sounded crazy, too.

"I need them for the bride I'm meeting . . ." She paused to glance at her watch. "In ten minutes."

Her hair slid over her shoulder and dipped into her smooth cleavage. He could look for those photos, he supposed. Invite her back inside. Kiss her mouth as he pulled her close until he felt her firm breasts against his chest. Run his hand up her smooth thighs and . . . "Not my problem." He shut the door in her beautiful, stunned face. He'd never slammed the door on a girl before, but he'd never felt so crazy before, either.

He let out a breath and leaned back against the door. He had a girlfriend. He'd been with Holly Ann longer than he'd been with anyone in the past. Guilt weighed on his conscience. Holly Ann was his girl. He should be all twisted up thinking of her, not some girl he didn't know. Not some girl with full pink lips and long tan legs. Not some girl named Becca Ramsey who heated his insides with thoughts of those long legs wrapped around his waist as he kissed her pink lips.

Chapter 2

THE HAVEN-HOLLOWELL WEDDING was the most anticipated event to take place in Lovett since Elvis Presley played at the Amarillo Municipal Coliseum in '55 .

Sadie Hollowell was practically Texas royalty and Vince . . . well, Vince Haven had served his country with honor and was a regular war hero. That alone made up for him being from the North. The fact that he'd bought the Gas and Go from his aunt Luraleen Jinks, and had remodeled the old convenience store so no one was afraid of catching ptomaine from the hot dog roller any longer, helped even further.

Unlike Elvis at the coliseum, the Haven-Hollowell wedding was to be a low-key, small affair with just close family and friends. Most everyone in town was disappointed not to get an invitation, but as Luraleen Jinks was fond of saying, "Sadie Hollowell always did think she was too good for her raisin's."

Bless her heart.

Vince's aunt had never bothered to hide her disapproval of Sadie, but she was willing to let bygones be bygones and even planned to bring a peace offering to the reception in the way of her famous Frito pie. The reception was not a potluck. It was a catered affair, but any Texas gathering was not complete without a good Frito pie, and Luraleen's was famous on the funeral circuit. For a wedding gift, Luraleen was even willing to write out the recipe on a nice card.

Frito pie was the furthest thing from Sadie's mind. No matter how famous. The bride-to-be pulled the wet towel from her hair, then hung it on the rack next to shower.

"What are your plans?" Vince asked his future wife.

"Wedding stuff," she answered as she stepped into her white panties and pulled them up legs still moist from her shower.

From the bedroom, the groom groaned is if in pain.

"You love it." She adjusted her breasts within her white bra, then reached for the hairbrush.

"About as much as I love a knee to the nuts." The old wood floor creaked beneath Vince Haven's feet as he rose naked from their bed.

"There's still Vegas." She brushed the tangles from her blond hair and added, "And the Little White Chapel."

"No. My sister did that," he reminded her as he walked into the bathroom. "It didn't really work out for her. She's happy now, but it took a while for her dumbass husband to step to the plate and make things right." He moved behind her and grasped her waist with his big hands.

Through the foggy mirror his light green eyes met hers and he added, "I'm still going to kick his ass someday. Might have to wait until he's done making a living with his body, though."

That was not an ass kicking that Sadie ever wanted to see. The "dumbass" Vince spoke about was professional hockey player Sam LeClaire. Sam was a premier athlete and stayed in top physical shape in order to score goals or drop his gloves to take on any and all opponents who were as big and bad as he. Vince was a retired Navy SEAL, as big and bad as any hockey player, with an additional set of "dispatching" skills.

"Behave while your sister and Sam and the boys are here for the wedding." Sadie had met Vince's sister, Autumn, and Sam twice now. The first time, Autumn and Sam and their son Conner had flown to Texas to meet Sadie and visit the JH Ranch where Vince now lived with her. The second time, Sadie and Vince had flown to Seattle to welcome Sam and Autumn's second son, Axel, into the world.

Vince pulled her back against the hard muscles of his chest. "Define 'behave.'"

"Don't antagonize Sam." Vince and his brother-in-law tolerated each other. Barely. No one held on to a grudge harder than Vince, and Sam didn't seem to have a real forgiving nature, either. The last thing she wanted was for their antics to ruin her wedding.

"Sam's a nancy-boy."

"Vince." She set the brush near the sink and stared down her fiancé in the mirror. "I mean it. You and Sam can't be in the same room without insulting each other, but I won't have you two ruining my wedding day. It's the only one I plan to have and no one is going to create havoc."

He slid his arms around her waist and pushed his erection into her behind. "It's the only one you're ever going to have."

"I don't want you and your friends getting drunk and fighting," she said, referring to the Junger brothers, who'd come to physical blows at their shooting range. The identical twins had duked it out over something so silly as who was the baddest superhero, Batman or Superman. The slugfest continued until Sadie's sister, Stella, got between the towering men and told them to knock it off.

"Blake doesn't drink these days, and since Beau knocked up your sister, he isn't knocking heads." He leaned his face down and kissed the top of her wet hair. "You always smell so good." If his erection wasn't already shoved against her butt, she would recognize the lust in his voice. "Let's go back to bed. I love you."

Through the mirror, she looked into his hot green eyes. She loved the way he said, "I love you," like it came from some emotional hiding place deep in his soul. Sometimes she still couldn't believe that this gorgeous man was hers. All hers. "I love you, too, but I'm not getting back in bed with you."

His big hands slid up her ribs to cup her breasts. "I can make you change your mind." His thumbs fanned her nipples pressed against the white nylon, and she was tempted. "You know I love kissing your thighs when you're just out of the shower," he added.

Real tempted. She did love the way Vince kissed between her thighs, and if she hadn't just spent the last two hours in bed, riding him like queen of the Tri-State Rodeo, she would have raced him back to bed, no matter who waited for her. "Becca's on her way over with some pictures of hair she's done for other weddings."

He dropped his hands and backed up as if he was a vampire and she had suddenly turned to silver. "The last time she touched your hair, it was shorter on one side."

"That was last year. She's gotten better, or so she says." She bit the corner of her mouth to keep from smiling and reached for a tube of moisturizer next to the sink. Vince and Becca had a love-hate relationship. Becca loved to chat with Vince and pour out her heart like he was the big brother she'd never had. Vince hated Becca's "drama" and avoided it as much as possible. "Besides, Becca's showing me her updos. No cutting or coloring involved."

He reached for the shower nozzles and turned them on. "If I'm still home when she gets here, tell her I'm gone."

Sadie squeezed the face lotion on the pads of her fingers, then rubbed it into her cheeks and forehead. "She loves you, Vince."

"She makes my brain burst with all her talk of hair and makeup and loser friends." He tested the water temperature with his hand. "She treats me like one of her girlfriends, and it's your fault."

Yes, she knew he blamed her. The second or third time that Sadie met Vince, they'd practically had sex inside the bride's room at the Sweetheart Palace Wedding Chapel. Before she'd even known quite how it happened,

Vince had her little bridesmaid dress around her waist and his warm hands and hot mouth on her hot places. "You started it that night. I didn't follow you."

He pushed the deep red shower curtain aside and stepped into the bath. "You're the one who got off, then left me in that room with a hard-on. I had blue balls for a week." He stuck the top of his head beneath the shower. "You were heartless."

Sadie chuckled and took out a tube of mascara. It was a good thing she'd left the room when she had because less than a minute after she'd grabbed her coat and partially run from the chapel, Becca had entered the bride's room to find Vince sitting in a salon chair, waiting for the "tent pole" in his pants to go down before he left, too. Vince was a big guy with big proportional parts. "I didn't want to scare the girl to death with my enormous hard-on," he'd told Sadie. So, he'd had to sit and wait while Becca sobbed about her last boyfriend, her backstabbing girlfriends, and her life in general. She'd mistaken Vince feeling trapped for feeling genuine interest and care about her heartache.

"Tell her I'm not home, honey" came from behind the curtain.

"I could go to hell for lying, Vince." She tried not to laugh. "You know I don't like to lie."

"Just this once." He stuck his head out, and water dripped down his nose and off his long black lashes. "Baby, I'll owe you big."

Wow, a honey *and* a baby. He was serious. "Don't antagonize Sam."

"Okay."

That was a little too easy. "Promise."

He held up one wet hand like a Boy Scout. "Promise."

BECCA SAT WITH her back straight and her knees to one side on the black-and-white cowhide sofa in the formal living room at the JH Ranch. She raised a cold glass of sweet tea to her lips and took a sip. "I had new photos taken to show you." The ice cubes rattled in the tall glass as she set it on the coffee table. "But they aren't ready yet." Nathan said his mother lied about putting the photographs in the mailbox. Daisy hadn't ever seemed like a liar to Becca. She was a professional. Why would she lie? Why would Nathan lie? It was crazy. Maybe the knock on his head had given him a concussion and memory loss.

"That's okay." Sadie pointed to a photo of a model with loose curls and a waterfall braid in back. "I like this one. It's pretty and informal."

"I like that one for you, too. It fits the wedding and your dress. It's relaxed and gorgeous with or without a veil." Sadie had chosen a simple filigree and pearl comb and single layer cathedral veil. "I can tuck your headpiece into the hair at your crown." The wedding was scheduled to take place in the big backyard, with the reception directly afterward in the bunkhouse. It wouldn't have been Becca's first choice in venues, but the more she knew Sadie, the more it fit her. And Vince, too. He was a no-fuss kind of man. He scowled and frowned a lot, but he was a regular sweetheart. "Is Vince around?"

Sadie shook her head and her gaze slid away. "No. He's not home. He's probably checking out my surprise wedding present. I think it's just about ready."

"I take it the surprise isn't a surprise."

Sadie shook her head and her straight blond hair fell over her bare shoulder and strap of her orange tank top. "He's having my mother's 1966 Cadillac restored down at Parrish's auto body shop."

"The long red car?"

Sadie smiled. "He had it painted red?"

Becca sucked in a breath and covered her mouth with her fingers. "You didn't know?"

Sadie leaned back against the cowhide sofa and laughed. "No." Light from the big antler chandelier shined in her blue eyes.

"I feel horrible. I thought it wasn't a surprise."

"It isn't." Sadie took a sip of her tea, then set the glass on an end table next to a portrait of her deceased daddy, Clive Hollowell. He looked as mean in the picture as he had in real life. "Vince doesn't know that I know, but you really can't haul a big car like that out of the barn without it being noticed." She set Becca's portfolio on the sofa between them. "Please don't let on that I know about the surprise. It's very sweet of him."

Becca nodded and took a drink of her tea. "He's a sweet guy." Sadie laughed and crossed one long leg over the other. She was a beautiful woman, and Becca figured that Sadie should thank her lucky stars and god or goddess of her choice that she resembled her beauty queen mother and not her grouchy daddy. "I think you'll like it." Although Becca didn't particularly care for old—or classic, rather—cars, the paint shone like a cherry apple in the sun.

"When did you see it?"

"Today." She took another drink then. "I had to run to Parrish American Classics before I came out here. Daisy took some photos for me, but there was mix-up and they weren't there. That's why I was a little late this afternoon." She was also a little late because she'd stood in Nathan Parrish's house, watching droplets of water run down his spine to the waistband of his underwear. She could have stood there all day and watched him blow water from his lips and shake his head and fling droplets around the kitchen. She could have watched him pull his T-shirt down his hard chest and flat belly just above his spiky belt a few more times, too. And for those few moments while she'd stood in his kitchen, she'd forgotten all about the photographs and her portfolio and that that she was a busy girl and time was money. She'd forgotten that she wasn't there to look into his eyes and breathe in the smell of soap and skin and the lingering hint of oil. So much for ignoring tingles and urges and lethal good looks.

"What color is the interior?"

Becca smiled. She knew it was white, but said, "I'm not going to ruin any more of Vince's surprise." Becca returned her glass to the table and grabbed a pink binder. "Do you know what Deeann wants me to do with her hair the day of the wedding?"

"I don't."

Deeann was Sadie's one and only bridesmaid, while

Stella was both maid of honor and the stand-in for their father. Sadie had asked her sister to walk her down the aisle. "I was thinking of doing a fishtail. Both those girls have long, straight hair, and I just thought something elegant and pretty." She flipped open her portfolio. "We don't want anything to take the attention from you."

"I don't know if that's possible. Stella's belly is huge and she waddles like a penguin these days."

"Has she outgrown her dress again?" Becca asked as the stairs to her right creaked. Stella walked toward them in a long black dress, looking amazingly like penguin.

"Are you okay?" Sadie asked her sister.

Stella waddled to a wingback chair and fell into it. "No." She shook her head, and the light from the antler chandelier glistened in the inky black strands of her hair. While Sadie was tall and fair, Stella was petite and had inherited her complexion from her Hispanic mother.

Concern wrinkled Sadie's brow. "Is there anything I can do for you?"

"My vagina hurts."

Becca sucked air between her teeth and the corners of her mouth turned downward. Stella Leon was close to thirty but looked younger. She stood just a tad over five feet, and the only thing she'd inherited from the father she shared with Sadie was Clive Hollowell's blue eyes.

"Oh. Well, I don't think there is anything I can do for your aching vagina."

"It's my cervix." Stella leaned her head back and closed her eyes. "I'm miserable."

She looked miserable, too. Becca wanted to have children one day, but not if it meant she had to walk around with a sore vagina and an aching cervix.

"We could try and pull the baby like a calf," Sadie offered. "I've got some experience with calving."

Stella opened her eyes. "No. Thank you." She rubbed her big belly and sighed. "Besides, she has to stay in there until after the wedding."

"When are you due?" Becca would guess she was overdue by a month, at least.

"Three weeks."

"Do you have a name picked out?"

"Not really. I want to name her Mercedes after Sadie, but I'd call her Mercy." She smiled at her stomach. "Beau wants to name her Olivia."

"That's pretty."

"Yeah, but it's a really common name." She glanced at her sister. "Have you seen Beau around?"

"No. I thought he wasn't supposed to get in from Dallas until tonight."

"He got an earlier flight and called me a while ago to say he's on his way to the ranch."

Becca stood with her portfolio and moved past a big stone fireplace with a horse painting on the mantel. "Sadie and I were discussing hair." She knelt by Stella's chair. "I thought you and Deeann would look pretty in fishtail braids."

Stella balanced the book on her belly. "Thank God. I thought Sadie was going to stick me with some hideous Texas hair."

Becca flipped a few pages to one of her most popular

prom hairdos. "Like this?" The model's hair had been set on big rollers, then backcombed in a half-up, half-down retro beehive.

"I actually like that." Stella pointed to the photo. "I used to wear an Amy Winehouse beehive once in a while, but it's too damn hot these days."

"It won't be hot in the bunkhouse," Sadie reassured her sister.

Becca looked up into Stella's face and her silky black hair. When things settled down, and the baby was born and Stella's vagina didn't hurt anymore, she'd love to have her as a hair model. Work about a ton of root pump in her hair and construct a stellar constellation circling her head.

The sound of a door closing near the rear of the big ranch house drew their attention to the hall. Becca took her portfolio and rose to her feet as Beau Junger moved toward them wearing a blue dress shirt with "Junger Securities" embroidered on his breast pocket. Like Vince, Beau was retired Special Forces. Becca couldn't recall which branch. Probably the one that camped out at the North Pole and wrestled polar bears for fun.

Vince and Beau were both big guys with ripped muscles and wide shoulders, but where she thought Vince was a sweetheart, Beau intimidated the heck out of her. Maybe it was his hard jaw and cold gray eyes that could freeze a person in place. At the moment, his cold eyes turned a warmer, softer gray, as he looked at the mother of his child.

"Hello ladies." He moved toward Stella and reached for her hand. "How are you feeling?"

"Okay."

"Her vagina hurts," Sadie told him as she rose to her feet. "And her cervix aches."

He looked from one sister to the other. "What does that mean? Is that in the baby book?" Becca stood a few feet behind Stella, and although she wasn't sure, she thought that perhaps the hard-as-nails, steely-eyed, ass-kicking security specialist looked a little afraid.

"It means you knocked up my little sister with a big baby." Sadie pointed at Stella, then dropped her hand to her side. "She's a small girl, and I've never seen anyone that big."

Beau kissed Stella's temple and put a hand on her belly. "I'm sorry, boots. I wish I could take the pain for you."

"So do I."

One corner of his mouth twisted in a smile. "How's the baby?"

"She kicked all night and I didn't get any sleep. My skin is so tight it itches like I'm covered in hives. I have to pee all the time and I'm just irritable."

He lowered his mouth to the side of her head and whispered something in her ear. Something warm and masculine that made Stella dip her head and her cheeks turn red. Something that only the two of them shared. "Stop," she told him.

"I missed you," Becca heard him whisper as he raised his face and smiled. "Excuse us." He glanced from Sadie to Becca. "It was nice to see you again."

"You too," she said as Beau led Stella out of the room and up the stairs. She turned and watched them leave.

She wanted that. She wanted a man to look at her the way Beau looked at Stella and the way she'd caught Vince looking at Sadie.

Becca was young. She was busy. There was lots of time to fall in love. Still, she wouldn't mind finding a man to whisper in her ear and make her laugh. A man who missed her when he went away and seemed desperate to return to her.

No. She wouldn't mind finding that at all, but for some reason, of all the men in Texas, all the men in the world, all the men she'd ever fantasized about falling madly for her at first sight, men like Zach Efron or Chris Pine, Nate Parrish and his blue eyes popped into her head. And that didn't make sense at all.

STELLA LAY SPREAD-EAGLE in the middle of the old wrought-iron bed while an oscillating fan stirred fine stands of her black hair. She wore a pink bra, and her huge belly hid most of her pink panties. She was more beautiful now than the first time Beau had seen her working behind a bar in South Beach, wearing a leopard bustier and a pair of tight leather shorts.

He picked up the open tub of cocoa butter lotion and dipped his hand inside. "You ready?"

"Mmm-hmm." She nodded and let out a tired sigh. "It's been five days. Make it good."

"You know I will." He sat and took her right foot in his hands. He rubbed the lotion into her arch and she let out a soft moan. If she wasn't so big with his child, he'd pull her against him and capture that moan in his mouth as he touched more than her foot. "You're beautiful," he said.

"I'm as big as cow."

"A beautiful cow."

She chuckled. "I'm fat."

"You're not fat." He massaged her ankle and the heel of her foot. Just over a year ago, Vince had contacted him and asked for a favor: find the younger sister that Sadie had never met. Until Clive Hollowell's death last year, Sadie hadn't known about Stella.

"I think I need one of those electric scooters like they have in Wal-Mart. I'll need it to zip to the bathroom at Sadie's wedding."

"There's probably a four-wheeler around here somewhere." Clive had never even hinted of his affair that had produced a second daughter. Now that Beau was about to have his own baby girl, he couldn't imagine not wanting her in his life every day. He couldn't imagine a circumstance in which he would raise one daughter and ignore the other. If Clive Hollowell were still alive, the two would have had a conversation about it, too.

"I think there's a four-wheeler in the barn, but I doubt I can climb on it."

He wasn't even going to let his mind recall all the times she'd climbed on him. He pressed his thumbs into her arch and thought of something else. Something boring like "How are the wedding plans?"

"Good. The event planner seems to have it all under control, although Becca seems to think the woman is lazy."

"Becca is one serious girl."

"She's kind of intense for a twenty-three-year old." Stella rose onto her elbows. "When I was twenty-three, I was singing in a crappy band at dive bars. I didn't have a clue what I was going to do with my life." A wrinkle pulled her brows together. "I just bounced from thing to thing, place to place. I'm such a slacker."

By the age of twenty-three, Beau had graduated sniper/scout school and been assigned to the First Recon Battalion, Fifth Marines. He and his twin, Blake, had always been competitive overachievers. "You're not a slacker." Stella had supported herself since graduating from high school. There had been no one to take care of her. "You've acquired a unique toolbox of skills and operate under many titles." No one had looked out for her, until now. "Currently, you're my baby incubator." The pregnancy certainly hadn't been planned, but neither he nor Stella was sorry for the unexpected surprise.

Stella laughed and her hair slid over one shoulder. "Sadie's worried that you knocked me up and won't marry me."

He raised a brow. "You still haven't told her?"

She shook her head. "I don't want anyone to think you had to marry me."

He didn't care what people thought. He'd asked Stella to marry him even before they'd found out she was pregnant. After they'd found out, he'd wanted to have a quickie ceremony at the justice of the peace. He wanted Stella and the baby covered on his insurance and under his protection. Stella had dug her heels in for a wedding with the white dress and flowers and a big cake.

They'd compromised. Something he didn't have a lot of experience doing, but with Stella, he was learning. She'd agreed to marry him, but only if he kept it secret from everyone, even his brother. He ran his hands up her ankle and massaged her calf. "When was the last time you had more than a passing acquaintance with a razor?"

Stella watched him from beneath her lowered lids. That look used to mean she wanted to make love. "The last time you shaved my legs for me." These days her nirvana came from a foot massage or a pint of Ben & Jerry's Vanilla Toffee Bar Crunch. Sometimes while she had both. "Who would have thought a big Marine like you would be so good at foot massage?"

Not him. "I told you I have a big set of skills in my toolbox." He never thought his life could be like this. He never thought he could love someone as much as he loved his wife.

BECCA SWEPT THE hair from around the salon chair
and threw it in the wastebasket near her station. Her last
cut and color had just left and she didn't have anything
booked for the rest of the day. Mondays were typically
light, and she needed to think up a way to put more clients in her book.

She set the broom next to the trashcan and reached
behind her to untie her black salon apron. The problem she
had getting new clients was that she had to work within
the contract she'd signed with Lily Belle's Salon and Day
Spa. Becca understood why Lily Matthews had strict pro-
cedures and rules regarding everything from employee
conduct to advertising. The salon attracted clientele who
expected a certain level of service. New clients without a
stylist preference were booked according to which stylist
was available. Sometimes that meant Becca was crazy-
busy. Other times, like today, she was done by two.

Several keys on a Hello Kitty ring sat on top of her salon cart next to her iPad. She tapped the touch screen and brought up her calendar. Tuesdays and Sundays were her days off and she swiped the screen until her Wednesday appointments appeared. A cut and color in the morning, root touchup, man's cut, and a stacked A-line. Men who came into the salon usually tipped well. Especially if she laughed at their jokes and wore something short. Like the military-inspired shirtdress she wore today. Navy blue with gold buttons down the front, the sleeveless dress hit Becca about mid-thigh and made her feel downright patriotic.

She planted her palms on the cart next to her iPad and read her week's appointments. Her hair fell over one shoulder and, as she scanned her packing list for Sadie and Vince's wedding, a weird little zap tickled the back of her ankle just above the heels of her navy pumps. For a split second, she thought her shoes might be too tight and cutting off her circulation, but then the little zap got hotter and slid up the backs of her calves and knees and thighs. It tingled her spine and raised the baby hair on the back of her neck. She wasn't holding a hair dryer with wet hands. Not like the time in beauty school when she'd given herself quite a shock and blown the breaker switches. No one had been able to figure out exactly how or why or—

"I found this mixed in with my mail." A familiar voice interrupted her scattered thoughts and a white folio plopped next to her iPad.

Becca looked over her shoulder and her breath caught

in her throat. Nate Parrish's starling blue eyes stared back at her from beneath his dark brows. His cheeks were a little red, like he'd been in the sun, and his hair disheveled as if he combed it with his fingers.

"My mother actually did leave your photos in the mailbox before she left town Friday." He shrugged and gave half a smile. A curve of one corner of his lips that was filled with enough charm to stop her heart like she'd been zapped with a lightning bolt. "They got stuck between my *Motor Trends* and *Muscle Car* magazines."

She turned and faced him, totally immune to guys with heart-zapping charm. "Thanks." She glanced past him to several other stylists and an esthetician who openly stared. She didn't blame them and returned her attention to Nate.

"You're welcome. It was kind of my fault you didn't have them for your meeting with Sadie Hollowell yesterday."

Yeah, she was immune to guys like that, but Lord love a duck, Nate Parrish was smoking hot. The kind that was effortless in the way he wore a navy T-shirt beneath a blue plaid shirt. They way he'd left it unbuttoned and loose and had rolled the sleeves up his forearms. He didn't have to try. He just was. "Did you drive all the way from Lovett to give them to me?"

"I had to test drive Sadie's Cadillac today and check for leaks." He lifted his gaze to her forehead and hair and said absently, "I had a few things in to do in Amarillo. You were on my list."

Yep. Totally immune. "Your to-do list?" But that didn't mean she couldn't flirt.

His gaze dropped to hers. "Do you want to be on my to-do list, Becca Ramsey?"

Flirting was harmless. She was a Southerner. A Texan. It was practically in her DNA. Flirting was just a conversation. "I'm sorry. I've got an appointment coming in about five minutes," she lied.

"Perfect. I only need four and a half." He raised his left wrist and checked his watch. "I've done some of my best work under pressure. In a broom closet, on the trunk of my car." He dropped his hand to his side. "Behind that big sign on top of the Beaver Den Buffet."

"The Beaver Den Buffet?" Surely she hadn't heard him right. "The neon 'All You Can Eat Y'all' sign?"

He grinned. "I took it as a challenge."

The way he said it, as if it was no big deal, was horrifying . . . and fascinating. In a morally deranged sort of way. "Wait." She held up a finger and lowered her voice to a scandalized whisper. "The sign with the cute beaver family rubbing their bellies? That sign?"

"Are there two neon beaver signs in Lovett?"

"You are so disturbed." She folded her arms beneath her breasts. "Folks eat there after Sunday church." She knew because her daddy had taken her to the Beaver Den on his every other Sunday. Until she'd been about thirteen and he'd moved to Houston to work the oil refineries. She'd hardly seen him after that.

"Folks eat there before Sunday church, too." He chuckled and rocked back on the heels of his Vans. "Best to get all the really good sins in before you have to repent."

"I don't think that's how repentance works." She was

pretty sure, anyway, but she couldn't think straight. Not with Nate's talk of sin and buffet and not when the memory of his bare chest and tan stomach were still so freshly vivid in her head. "I fear for your immortal soul."

"That's real sweet of you."

The skin on his belly so hard and tight, thoughts of love bites along his happy trail popped into her head. "Thank you. I try to be sweet to everyone. I was raised on it." There was nothing wrong with sexual thoughts. They were normal and natural, but she never acted on them until she fell in love. Which was usually after five dates. That was kind of her rule for herself. Love and a five-date minimum.

"Now I feel bad."

"Now? Now you feel bad but didn't when you were . . . were . . ." She lifted a hand and gestured toward him. "When you were desecrating the Beaver Den?"

"You're funny." He chuckled and shook his head. "I never had sex with anyone behind the beaver family at the all-you-can-eat buffet. I just always thought someone should."

"What?" Her brows lowered. "I'm confused."

"I wasn't serious. I was just joking with you."

Becca didn't always get boy humor. "Oh."

"You look disappointed."

Was she? Maybe.

"If you're disappointed, we could always make it true." He leaned forward and said next to the side of her head, "No one else has to know. Just you and me and cute beavers." The warmth of his breath was still caught in her hair when he leaned back and smiled, all smooth charm and effortless good looks. "Think of it as camping above a restaurant."

"As romantic as that sounds," she said past the sudden hitch in her chest, "I'll have to pass."

He raised a hand to his chest like she'd broken his heart. He opened his mouth to say something but his aunt Lily called out to him and he turned to her.

"Has hell frozen over?" Lily asked as she walked toward them wearing a tight yellow tank dress that hugged her slight baby bump. "I don't think you've been in my salon since my grand opening. You or your dad."

"It stinks in here." He opened his arms and embraced his aunt. "It smells like face cream and nail polish and toxic hair spray." He was taller than Lily by several inches. "The fumes will probably shrink my balls."

Lily laughed and pulled back to look up into his face. "Your balls are safe, Nathan. Tucker comes in all the time and there is nothing wrong with that man's balls," she said, referring to her husband, Deputy Tucker Matthews.

"Obviously." He dropped his arms. "How are you feeling?"

"Still sick as a dog every morning."

"You're like my mom. She was sick with Rosie." While Lily and Nathan swapped morning sickness stories, Becca let her gaze surreptitiously slide down the back of his plaid shirt. His pants weren't necessarily baggy, but they were by no means tight. In Lovett, some men wore their Wranglers extremely tight to show off a bulge. And sometimes, not a very impressive bulge, either. Normally, Becca didn't care for tight pants on a man, but at the moment, she wouldn't mind if Nate's jeans were a little more butt hugging, truth be told.

"At the risk of breathing toxic fumes and shrinking your balls, what brings you in today?" Lily asked. "Finally going to let me wax that uni-brow?"

Becca bit her lip and raised her gaze. She wasn't the only one who'd noticed that Nate could benefit from attention to his brows.

As if he read her mind, Nate glanced behind him and frowned. "I brought some photos Mom took for Becca."

Lily looked past her nephew. "I didn't know you knew Nathan."

"We just met when I went searching for my new photos to show Sadie," Becca told her boss.

"Has Sadie chosen an updo for herself and her bridesmaids?"

Lily was Sadie's hairstylist. She was talented with scissors and color, but she didn't enjoy occasion hair. Not like Becca. "Sadie wants loose, sexy curls tucked into a waterfall and the girls are each going to have a fishtail braid."

"That should be fairly easy for you." Lily gave her a confident smile. "Marilee and I will be there if something comes up."

Lily and Marilee were doing the makeup and anything else the bridal party might need or want.

"Are you finished for the day?" Lily asked.

Becca looked up at Nate through the corners of her eyes. "Yes."

"You little liar," Nate said through a smile.

If Lily heard her nephew, she didn't ask questions. "And you're off tomorrow. Right?"

"Yes." Becca couldn't help the smile she returned to Nate. "Tuesdays and Sundays are my days off."

"Then let's get together Wednesday when you're free. We should trade notes and make sure we have everything we'll need for Sadie's big day."

Becca nodded. "Okay."

Lily turned to her nephew. "Do you have time for some iced tea?"

"I never have time for that sweet crap you drink, but I'll take you for a spin in Sadie's wedding present."

"The Coupe Deville?"

"Finished putting in the water hose yesterday."

"Let me get my purse and a scarf so my hair doesn't get messed." Nate watched Lily move toward her office, then turned back to Becca. She expected him to comment on her little white lie. Instead he asked, "What are you doing tomorrow?"

"Not camping out at the Beaver Den, that's for sure."

Humor pinched the corners of his blue eyes. "Drive out to the lake with me."

"Lake Meredith?" With Nate Parrish. Or any guy really. She was busy. She had a lot to do. Like planning how to promote herself and do laundry. "I don't know."

He smiled like he was harmless. "No camping or beavers involved. I promise I can keep my hands to myself if you can."

Just a drive? It sounded innocent enough. Did she

trust him to keep his hands to himself? Did she trust herself? What would she wear?

When she didn't answer right away, he took a step back and put his hands in his front pockets. "You don't work tomorrow. I have the day off, so I just thought . . ." He shrugged and his brows knitted together over his blue eyes as if he was confused about something. "Maybe some other time."

"Yes," she said before she could talk herself out of it.

He took another step back. "I'll text you next week, then."

"No." She shook her head. "I'll go with you to the lake tomorrow." A drive. A simple drive. She'd be gone a couple of hours, then back home. There was no harm in a simple drive.

A smile of pleasure curved his mouth and cleared his brow. "Good." He lifted his gaze as Lily walked toward them with her scarf and purse in hand. "Bring your swimsuit in case we want to get wet."

Now, that didn't sound so innocent, and the warm rush spreading up her chest from the pit of her stomach was anything but harmless.

HE'D TOLD HER he'd keep his hands to himself. He was a guy who could keep his word, but, God, he wanted to touch her. From the minute she'd jumped into his truck wearing a bright yellow bikini under a pair of jean shorts and tight white tank top, he wanted to run his hands all over Becca Ramsey. During the hour-long drive to the lake, he wanted to reach across the bench seat and slide his palm to the side of her bare knee and up the inside of her thigh. If he hadn't promised . . . if he didn't have a girlfriend down in Dallas . . . if it didn't feel strangely important, somehow, that he not pressure her or risk pushing her away, he would have touched more than her hand when he'd helped her onto the boat his parents kept docked during the summer.

"I haven't been up here for a long time." Becca stood in the center of the twenty-three-foot Malibu Wakesetter with her back to him and her hands inching her shirt up her bare waist. She pulled the tank top over her head, and her ponytail brushed her shoulders. The hot afternoon sun bounced off the water and metal board racks, and behind his mirrored sunglasses, Nate watched her shorts slide down her long legs to her bare feet. God, sitting there in the captain's seat, in the Texas heat, was better than drinking cold beer in a strip bar. Nothing fake about her, and he didn't have to worry about breaking a twenty. Then it got even better when she bent over and picked up her shorts. He about popped a blood vessel in his eyeballs but the pain was worth the view. One side of her bikini bottoms slid over the curve of her smooth butt and he got a nice view of under boob. God, he loved under boob. He should feel bad for staring, but he didn't. Then she rose and slid the tip of her index finger beneath the elastic leg of her bottoms. She snapped it back in place and he felt it between his legs. Beneath his sternum, too. "Your family must come here a lot," she said.

"Yeah." He'd come to the lake for the first time with

his mother and father at the age of fifteen. "I don't get up here that much anymore."

She turned and tossed her clothes on the empty seat. The snap to his chest and nuts turned to a hard thump, and he had to remember his promise before he jumped to his feet and jumped on Becca. A thin bow tied her top together between her cleavage, and two perfectly centered nipples poked at the yellow triangles of her bikini top. Nate had spent many years in the study of breasts. He'd done his homework. He'd used the Internet in his parents' house for more than school book reports. Even before his first sexual experience, he'd known pretty much all there was to know about the female body. If he had a question that he couldn't find the answer to through his research, he asked his father. He could talk to his dad about anything. Sex. Cars. Fishing.

"I thought you didn't like iced tea," she said as she reached for the solo cup in the holder.

"I don't." At the moment, he couldn't recall ever having a conversation about tea with Becca. He must have, and she'd remembered. "But you're a Texan so I figured you did."

"Don't tell me you made this." She took a drink, and her blue gaze met his over the bottom of her red plastic cup.

"My grandmother. I stopped by her house before I picked you up." Even if he knew nothing about women, he'd know that Becca was perfect. Perfect butt and perfect breasts. Round and tight in all the right places. Smooth and flat in others. Beautiful face and hair and skin. Perfect little mound beneath her bikini bottom. He wanted to touch her. To slide his hand between her soft legs and kiss her breasts, but as much as he wanted to touch her, he wanted to know her, too .

As much as possible, he pushed aside thoughts of sex and listened to her talk about her life and her plans for the future. She moved to the front of the boat and sat her perfect butt on the right bench seat. She stretched her legs out in front of her and one arm along the side. With her face tilted toward the sun, she told him about her past and a series of bad boyfriends.

"I'm a magnet for guys who cheat on me," she said, her voice all lazy and relaxed.

Guys like him. Guys who had a girlfriend but couldn't seem to remember that when she wasn't around. Nate sat on the seat across the narrow bow, and as much as he tried not to think about putting his mouth on her body, waves conspired against him. Each time another boat passed, the waves grew bigger. Each dip and bob tortured him with the firm bounce of her breasts, and even if he could tear his gaze away, she constantly lifted her hand to make sure she was still tucked safely behind those two yellow triangles.

"My mom attracts cheaters, too. It must be genetic."

If he'd meant to keep his hands to himself like he'd promised, why in the fuck had he thought getting her alone in the middle of a lake was a good idea? In a bikini?

"My daddy was the worst."

When he'd entered his aunt's salon yesterday, he hadn't meant to stick around and talk to Becca. He'd certainly never meant to ask her to take a drive with him, but she'd looked so beautiful and sexy and he'd had an overwhelming desire to see her again.

Nate rose and ripped his T-shirt over his head. He had a raging hard-on beneath his board shorts. The shorts were baggy, but if she dropped her gaze to his lap, she couldn't help but notice. He had a girlfriend down in Dallas and a girl on his boat he wanted dive down on. Instead he jumped to his feet, climbed onto the seat, and dived deep into the water. He resurfaced with a loud "Whaaaaa," as the cold water shrank his balls, and the thought of doing Becca receded enough that he began to relax.

"How cold is it?" she asked as she peered over the side at him.

"Freezing," he answered so she wouldn't dive in with him.

"Good!" She climbed onto the seat and jumped in. "Whaaaaa," she shouted as she surfaced and swam toward him. "This feels good." Beads of water slid into the crease of her lips, and her long legs kicked behind her.

Without a word, Nate swam to the back of the boat and climbed onto the deck. He needed to go. He needed to get her home. Away from his reach. She didn't seem to notice his torture. Not as he drove the boat back to the dock, and not as he drove her home.

In the parking lot of her apartment complex, he breathed a sigh of relief. "Thanks for driving up to the lake with me," he said as he opened the passenger door for her.

"I had a good time." She grabbed her purse and slid out of the truck. "I haven't relaxed like that in a long time."

At least one of them had been relaxed. She slipped past him, and the front of her damp tank top brushed his arm. His brain went blank and he reached for her. He slid a hand to the back of her neck beneath her still wet ponytail. Without any thought of his promise, he lowered his face to hers and coaxed her lips apart with his mouth. He kissed her like he'd kissed dozens of girls in his life. Soft at first, then teasing her into a chase of tongues. Her wet mouth tasted good, and within a matter of seconds it became unclear who was teasing and who was chasing. Who was giving and taking, and who was in control.

Kissing her was a mistake. He knew it as his hand found her waist and he pulled her into him. He knew it as the front of her damp shirt chilled his skin through his T-shirt. And he knew it as he felt the weight of her breasts pressed against him and as her pebble-hard nipples stabbed his chest. He knew it but he wanted to make that mistake with her. A hot, messy mistake with her naked skin sliding against his as he slipped between her legs and entered her wet, wanting body.

He pulled back and looked into her lazy gaze. His breath brushed her cheek as he struggled to pull air into his lungs like he'd just run a marathon. Her deep blue eyes looked up at him, open and honest and with nothing to hide. Not like him. He wasn't open and honest and was purposely keeping important details of his life from her.

For the second time that day, the third time since he'd laid eyes on her, Nate moved away from the beautiful mistake he'd give his left nut to make.

Chapter 4

THE WEDDING OF Vince Haven and Sadie Hallowell was scheduled for seven p.m. beneath the yellow rose arbor at the JH Ranch. The temperature had dipped to eighty degrees, and close friends and family filled several rows of white chairs set up for the occasion.

At seven on the dot, Ginger Pratt and Margo Corrigan, from First Baptist on Third and Houston, struck up the music. The harp and violin drifted on a warm Texas breeze and the wedding planner motioned for the ring bearer, Vince's young nephew Conner, to start down the aisle. Next, she waved for the bridesmaid and best man. Deeann took her cue and tucked her hand inside of the elbow of Blake Junger's black tuxedo jacket. They stepped from the main house and started down the grassy path strewn with rose petals. Deeann's blue chiffon dress fluttered about her knees and her red braid glistened in the evening sunlight.

Stella Leon Junger took a breath and let it out slowly. She wasn't the one getting married, but her nerves made her stomach tight.

"Do you need to use the bathroom?"

Stella laughed and looked up at her sister. "No." Sadie was stunning in her simple white gown and long veil tucked into the pearl comb Becca Ramsey had placed in her blond hair. "I just went."

"That doesn't mean anything. You have to go about every five minutes!" Sadie let out a rush of breath and puffed out the tulle in front of her face. "Sorry. I'm nervous."

"I'm here with you." Stella switched her bouquet of blue hydrangeas and white sweet peas and reached beneath her sister's veil to take her hand. "I love you, big sister."

Sadie looked down and squeezed her hand. "I love you, little sister."

The wedding planner signaled them and the girls walked down the aisle, sweaty palm against sweaty palm, to Pachelbel's Canon in D. The beautiful mix of violin and harp drifted on the slight breeze, and tears stung the backs of Stella's eyes. It wasn't just that she was pregnant and prone to sudden bouts of emotion. A year ago, she hadn't known her life would be this good. In just twelve months, she'd found her sister and the love of her life.

Her gaze searched the front few rows, past Vince's sister and husband and their two boys, to Beau. His gray eyes were filled with a look she recognized, the same combination of love and joy that filled her own chest.

The sweet smell of roses filled the air and her nose as

she took her place beneath the arbor. Vince looked nervous, but sure. As Sadie promised to love Vince for the rest of her life, his sister, Autumn, softly wept from the front row. Her husband, Sam, wrapped an arm around her shoulders while he held his sleeping toddler in his free arm. His hand caressed her bare shoulder in a way that was both loving and familiar.

Then it was Vince's turn to say his vows and Sadie's turn to cry as he promised he would love and cherish her forever. He slid a nice-size diamond on Sadie's finger, raised her veil, and kissed her for the first time as man and wife.

The ceremony was short and poignant. Afterward, Beau helped Sadie onto a four-wheeler and drove her to the barn, where Daisy Parrish took more wedding photos. She'd been there all day, snapping pictures while Sadie dressed and the super perky Becca Ramsey worked magic on all their hair. Stella liked Becca. She seemed thoughtful and had a genuine love and caring for Vince and Sadie, but her energy was exhausting. Or perhaps Stella thought so because she easily tired these days and was generally exhausted all the time.

While wedding guests were served hors d'oeuvres in the long cookhouse made of cinder block and stucco, Daisy took photos of the wedding party in the hayloft. Lily and another stylist touched up lips and cheeks, while Becca, in a little floral dress and cowboy boots, fussed over Sadie's hair and tucked it into the pearl comb after she'd removed the veil. Vince and Sadie posed with pitchforks and on hay bales and looking out the loft door at the JH. Once Stella had done her part, she and Beau left to find a bathroom. They moved down the stairs with Beau directly in front in case she "toppled forward." At the bottom, she moved wrong and pulled a muscle at the bottom of her belly.

"Ouch." She paused and sucked in a breath.

Beau turned, worry etching the corners of his gray eyes. "Is it the baby?"

"No. I pulled something." The pain subsided and Beau helped her onto the four-wheeler. He drove her to the closest bathroom in the bunkhouse, then on to the cookhouse. Hunger pangs burned her stomach next to her heartburn, and she didn't know if she could stand two more weeks of feeling like a whale with bladder issues.

"You still okay?" Beau stood behind her and softly rubbed her belly.

With her mouth stuffed with little chicken kabobs, she nodded. Next, she nibbled on stuffed mushrooms and cucumber cups stuffed with crab. Vince's aunt had brought something she called Frito pie, but Sadie passed. If water gave her heartburn, Frito pie would burn a hole in her esophagus.

At the far end of the cookhouse, Conner LeClaire ran across the polished floor, then dropped to his knees and slid about twenty feet.

"Stop that, Conner," his mother called out to him. "You're going to hurt yourself and someone else."

He completely ignored his mother as if he suffered from convenient hearing loss.

Autumn called out one more time, then said something to her husband standing by her side.

"Conner." He set Axel on his feet and said, "Your mother is talking to you."

"Just one more time," he called out over his shoulder.

"Okay," Sam said at the same time his wife said, "No!"

Axel took off after his older brother. He was fast but he wasn't coordinated. He fell and plowed into several other kids, knocking them over like bowling pins. Those little nuts didn't fall far from the tree, Stella thought as she watched the chaos. They were like their father, famous for knocking around opposing hockey players and getting bloody.

Boys, Stella thought as Autumn and Sam did damage control. No one got hurt, but Stella was glad she was having a girl.

"What have you done to little Stella?" Beau's twin, Blake, asked as he and his girlfriend, Natalie, moved toward them.

"Made sure she couldn't run very far." The twins laughed, an identical deep sound of amusement. They tipped their heads back at identical angles and smiled identical smiles. As much as the two were identical, they were different, too. Stella didn't have any problem telling them apart anymore.

"How are you feeling?" Natalie asked her.

"Tired. Huge." She rubbed the top of her belly as heartburn gripped beneath her sternum. The baby kicked as if she felt the heartburn, too.

"Are your feet swollen? That's one thing I did not enjoy about pregnancy."

Natalie had a cute little girl named Charlotte. Stella had met them both twice now. "They look like bricks."

Natalie groaned. "I don't know which is worse. Sore, swollen feet or the heartburn."

The two women chatted about third trimester pregnancy and compared horror stories until Vince burst into the cookhouse with his bride thrown over his shoulder. Everyone broke into applause and the twin brothers whooped and whistled.

"Cryin' all night! Put me down, Vincent." When he did, Sadie smoothed her hair, then punched her husband in the arm. Stella laughed, and her stomach ached from the simple exertion. With a huge grin on his face, Vince bent his new wife over his arm and kissed her in front of the small, cheering crowd. Stella laughed so hard this time, her bladder squeezed past its limit and she felt warm liquid run down her legs. Horrified, she bent forward as far as possible and looked at the puddle between her jeweled sandals. "Beau!" She glanced over her shoulder and pulled on his sleeve.

"What, honey?" With laughter still on his lips, he looked into her face. "Do you need to go to the bathroom again?"

"I think I already went." Her cheeks got hot and she squeezed her legs together to stop the flow. She was so embarrassed she wanted floor to open up so she could fall through. She wanted to hide behind her big husband or maybe she could fake like she'd spilled some water. "I think I peed myself." This time she hadn't even felt like she had to go, and she always felt like she had to go lately. "A lot." More than she'd been able to urinate in quite a while, and this time no matter how hard she squeezed her legs, the puddle grew bigger. She grasped Beau's hard forearm beneath his sleeve and her eyes rounded. Her belly got tighter and she sucked in a breath. "I don't think it's pee. I think my water broke."

THE SUN HAD turned into a flaming orange ball in the darkening sky by the time Becca packed her car and headed to the barn to grab the long, gauzy veil that Sadie had forgotten in the loft.

The wedding had been elegant and beautiful, like Sadie herself. Everything had been working according to plan . . . until Stella's water broke and all hell broke loose. Beau rushed with her from the cookhouse, practically running with Stella in his arms, her protests hanging in the air. Sadie hurried after them, issuing orders. "Everyone stay and have a good time. I'm going to the hospital. We're having a baby." Vince laughed at the sudden chaos, then followed his wife out the door. The wedding hadn't exactly gone off as planned, but it was certainly memorable. Most of the guests had stayed for several hours, but now the ranch was quiet except for the LeClaires, who had settled in the main house with popcorn and *Cars 2*.

The soft nicker of horses filled the barn as the heels of Becca's cowboy boots thumped on the wooden stairs. She climbed the steps to the loft and easily found the gossamer veil on a hay bale. The sound of a car driving toward the house, instead of away, drew her attention to the open hayloft doors.

Headlights cut through the dusky shadows of night

and she moved to the edge to look down at the red Cadillac with its white top up. The vehicle pulled to a stop beneath her and the engine died. She felt a little tug at the bottom of her heart as the door swung open and Nate Parrish stepped out. His bright white T-shirt shone in the deepening shadows of night like he'd smeared his chest and shoulders with glow-in-the-dark paint. She didn't have to see him clearly to know a spiky belt held up his loose jeans. He glanced around as if he'd expected the party to be in full swing. She didn't have to see his face or feel the touch of his hands on her waist or his mouth on hers to feel a shiver brush up her spine. Her body remembered whether she wanted to remember or not.

Becca's nerves had been jumping all day in anticipation of that long red car pulling up to the JH. In anticipation of seeing his handsome face and hearing his voice, not that she knew if he'd even talk to her.

He pulled his cell phone from his front pocket and the lighted screen lit up his hand as he punched in several numbers. Becca hadn't seen Nate since he'd taken her to the lake several days ago, and he hadn't tried to contact her in any way. She'd thought they'd had a good time, but she'd obviously been confused about that.

He held the phone to his ear for several moments, then tossed it into the Cadillac.

She'd thought his kiss had been filled with passion. White-hot desire and raw need, but she'd obviously been confused about that, too.

Several strands of golden hay fell from the toes of her boots and he looked up. For a split second, his gaze met hers, and instead of calling out to him, she backed away from the door.

One thing she wasn't confused about, though, was her feelings for him. She liked him and wanted to see more of him. A whole lot more. So much so that the sound of his shoes on the wooden stairs made her suck in her breath and forget to let it out. She turned as his dark silhouette appeared, and with the each step he took toward her, his handsome face became more visible.

"Where is everyone?" he asked, his deep voice cutting through the darkness.

"Stella's having her baby. Vince and Sadie left to be with her." She clutched the veil to the front of her floral wrap dress. "Folks stayed around for a while but left already."

"You're kidding."

She shook her head. "No."

"My mother didn't call and let me know not to drive all the way out here."

And of course he hadn't driven out to see her. While she'd been obsessing about that kiss, he hadn't given her a thought. "I guess in all the chaos she forgot." She was hurt by his disinterest even as her nerves made her stomach all squishy. "I'm just leaving. It's getting late and I have . . ." She stopped and bit the corner of her bottom lip. She'd chatted a lot the day at the lake. He hadn't seemed to mind, but she must have been confused about that, too.

"What?" He gently pulled the veil from her hands and tossed it on the hay bale. "What do you have to do?"

She didn't know. She couldn't remember. "Leave."

"I think you should stay for a while yet." He took her hands in his and pulled her a step closer to him.

"Why?"

"Because I can't stop thinking about you." He slid her palms up the front of his shirt to the back of his neck. His cool, fine hair tickled her fingers.

She didn't believe him. If he couldn't stop thinking about her, why hadn't he tried to see her? "Right."

A dark brow rose up his forehead. "You don't believe me?"

"No." But she wanted to. Really really bad.

"It's the truth." He settled his hands in the curve of her waist. "I can't stop thinking about kissing you and I think we should do it again."

"I don't think we should," she told him, but she didn't step out of his grasp. Not yet.

"I think I should change your mind." Slowly, as if giving her a choice to stop him, he lowered his mouth to hers. The brush of his lips stole what little breath was left in her lungs. The second she opened her mouth beneath his, he kissed her like he meant to take her choice away. If she thought the last kiss had been filled with raw passion, this time Nate showed her that she hadn't a clue. This time it was filled with so much scorching need, she didn't think to stop him when he slid his hands up her ribs. Through her thin dress and lace bra, he cupped her breasts and she took his deep moan into her mouth. He touched and teased her, and nipples turned hard with the sweet ache of pleasure and the pain of wanting more.

She should stop him while she still could. It was the

right thing to do. If she stretched the five-date minimum rule, she could call the day at the lake a date. But that was still just one date. Not five.

Instead, she clung to him as his tongue chased hers and his hands pulled her dress apart, and he pushed her bra down her chest. His warm palms cupped her breasts and he brushed her nipples with the tips of his fingers. His touch made her feel restless with wanting more.

He pulled back and gasped for air. His gaze dropped to his hand. "Tell me you want this."

She licked her dry lips. She did. She wanted it bad, but admitting it would mean disregarding her rule of love before sex.

"Tell me you want it right here. Right now." He lowered his face once more and fed her a wet kiss before he slid his mouth to her neck just below her ear. "I hear there was a wedding today. It only seems fitting that you say I do."

"Mmm."

"You're beautiful and perfect and I want to put my mouth on your breasts." His grasp tightened. "Tell me you want it, too."

God help her, she did.

"The other day at the lake, I wanted to do this and a lot more. A *lot* more. I can't recall ever wanting anything the way I wanted to kiss you and touch you and chew your bikini off."

"I didn't think you liked me." She ran her hands over his shoulders and arms, and her fingers through his hair. "I thought I might have annoyed you."

"Oh, you did." His soft laughter brushed the shell of her ear. "But only because I wanted to jump on you. Now it's worse. I don't want to jump on you, Becca Ramsey.

Her hands stilled.

"I want to make love to you." He slid his open mouth to the hollow of her throat. "Tell me you want it, too. Tell me you're going to die if I don't touch you all over. Tell me you're going to die if you don't touch *me* all over, too. I've never asked a girl to tell me she wanted me as bad as I want her, but I'm asking 'cause I got a feeling I'm going to want more from you. I want more than sex. Tell me you want to make love."

There was only thing left for her to say. "I do."

For the second time that day, chaos broke out at the JH. Shoes flew and clothes dropped to the hay. A hot fury of hands and mouths touched and tore at each other. Becca ran her palms over the defined balls of Nate's biceps and corded muscles of forearms. The guy lifted engines instead of weights and it showed in tight skin and beautiful hard body. She shoved her stomach into his and felt the rigid length of his hot erection against her crotch. "I do, Nate," she gasped. "I really really do."

Naked, he pressed her to his hot chest and kissed her soul-deep and walked backward with her to the bale of hay. He sat with her standing between his legs, then pulled her closer until she felt his hot breath brush her breast. His gaze looked up into her and he took her nipple into his wet mouth. His eyes closed and his groan vibrated his lips and tongue. Waves of pleasure rolled through her and she ran her fingers through his hair. He knew what he was doing, stabbing and licking and softly sucking each breast until she wanted to beg him to stop even as she wanted to beg him to never stop. As if he read her mind, he looked up at her and slid his hand between her legs. "I love that I make you wet." A sexy smile curved his lips and lit his sleepy blue eyes. "You want me inside."

She nodded. "I do."

He grabbed a condom out of the wallet he'd tossed on the hay bale and tore at the package. "I want you to straddle my lap." He rolled the lubricated latex over the spongy head of his penis and down the thick, long shaft to his dark pubic hair. "No need for both of us to get hay in our ass." He reached for her waist and she climbed on him. Through the growing darkness inside the loft, his gaze sought hers, intense and heavy with the same lust that wanted him inside her. He paused to kiss her breasts before he positioned his erection between her legs and grasped her thigh. He pushed her down as he thrust up, and in one smooth stroke, he buried himself deep inside like a hot knife. His grasped tightened on her thigh and her back arched. She cried out in pain and the most exquisite pleasure she'd ever felt in her life.

"Damn," he said between clenched teeth. "You feel good. Hot and so good." He lifted her, then thrust upward once more. "Ride me."

Her hand grabbed his shoulders and she did as he'd asked. She rode him like he was the bull at Gilley's. "Don't stop," she said through breathy moans. "Just don't stop."

He pumped into her, building the pleasure deep between her legs. "Not a chance. You're a sweet girl."

At the moment she didn't feel like a sweet girl. She felt like the kind of girl who wanted to bury her face in Nate's neck and bite him hard.

He slid one hand to the place where their bodies joined and touched her there without missing a beat of his pumping hips. "Your little muffin's so sweet." Another deep groan spilled past his lips "So good."

He's a groaner, she thought just as the first wave of orgasm heated her skin, radiating outward from the hot coil getting tighter with every stroke. "Nate," she called out as he plunged faster. Harder, as his fingers stayed with her, turning her mindless to anything but the pleasure racing through and rushing across her skin, until she opened her mouth to scream. The sound died in her throat as wave after luscious wave rolled through her. Her muscles pulsed and contracted, gripping him hard. His heavy breathing stirred the hair stuck to her damp throat and he shoved into her one last time as his hands gripped her thighs.

He whispered her name and crushed her to his chest as if he wanted to absorb her into his chest. "Sweet baby Jesus," he whispered as Becca saw spots behind her closed eyelids. She'd never had such an intense orgasm, didn't recall it being so good, and she feared she might faint from pleasure overload. He remained deeply embedded in her body when he looked up at her and smiled. "That was good, Becca. Do you know how good you are?"

Instead of admitting that she didn't, she returned his smile. "Do you know how good you are?"

"Of course. Come home with me and let me do that some more."

She didn't have to work tomorrow. She could stay awake until the sun came up. "Do you need a ride home?"

"I do." His penis stirred within her. "Tell me you want to spend all night in bed with me."

"Yes." She nodded. "Yes, I do."

Chapter 5

NATE SQUINTED AGAINST the morning light piercing his eyes through the small bathroom window. He turned on the shower, then stepped inside. In the kitchen, Becca was making pancakes and juice, giving him just enough time to wash up.

Last night had been the best sex of his life. Every orgasm felt like it had been ripped from the center of his core. The second, third, and fourth had been just as intense as the first.

He hurried and scrubbed his hair and body. He wanted more time with her before she left. And he especially wanted to watch her make pancakes while wearing his old "Parrish Classics" T-shirt.

He felt more than just *like* for Becca and he wanted more from her in return. He wasn't sure exactly what that meant, only that he wanted more.

He dried his skin and stepped into a clean pair of

cargo pants. More of her smiles and laughter and bad date stories. More touches and kisses and more of her sweet, sweet body. He wrapped a towel around his neck and walked bare-chested from the bathroom and into the kitchen. The room was empty and the still frozen juice sat on the counter alongside the box of pancake mix. She hadn't started to cook. Good, that meant more time for him to watch. "Becca?" he called out.

"In here."

He followed her voice and raised the towel to the side of his head. "What are you doing?" he asked as he moved the living room, but the question hung in the air, unanswered. His feet came to an abrupt halt and his hand dropped to his side. Holly Ann sat in his father's old recliner, her arms across her chest and her foot bobbing with anger.

"You're back in town." He didn't want to look at Becca. He'd rather shoot himself than see the anger she must be feeling right about now.

Holly Ann's brows lowered over her brown eyes. "Obviously, Nate."

"How long have you been here?" He could fix this. He could, but he just had to figure out how.

"Long enough." Her foot stopped. "Don't you think you should have told me that I've been replaced?" And started again. "Or is this just a hookup that I wasn't supposed to find out about?"

"No." He finally forced himself to look at Becca, sitting on the couch, dressed in her clothes from the previous night. She didn't look mad, just deeply hurt. "Ah shit."

Her blue eyes filled with moisture and she rose to her feet. "I told you that I don't like cheaters," she said, and grabbed her purse. "I told you and you still used me to cheat on your girlfriend."

"It's not like that, Becca."

"Right."

He held a hand toward her as he watched her walk to front door. "I can explain." But he needed to deal with Holly Ann. He needed to resolve things with his girlfriend first.

"Don't come near me ever again." Becca ducked her face as a tear slid from her bottom lashes.

Nate curled his hands into fists to keep from reaching for her as she walked out the door.

"I can't believe you've cheated on me." Holly Ann rose and planted her hands on her hips. "If you wanted out, you should have told me."

"When?" He lifted a hand and dropped it to his side. "You've been out of town for months."

"You know I love you and that I was coming back."

"If you really loved me, you wouldn't have been able stay away so long." He took a breath and let it out slow. "Did you really want me to end things over the phone or by text?"

"It would have been better than walking in here and seeing your hookup in one of your T-shirts."

"Becca isn't a hookup."

"Then what is she, Nate?"

"More."

"How much more?"

Good question.

She swallowed hard. "I deserve an answer."

Maybe she did. The problem was that he didn't have a real good answer. Not for her or himself.

JACK PARRISH WALKED past his secretary of twenty years, busily directing calls and typing with her long fingernails at the same time. "Give me half a minute, then put him though, will ya, Penny honey?"

"You know I'll do anything when you call me honey," she answered without pause.

Yeah, he knew. He walked into his office and closed the door behind him, shutting out the whine of spinning sanders and the grind of metal on metal. He moved behind his desk and sat in a comfy new chair Daisy had wheeled in just last week. It was the first new chair he'd had since taking over taken the business twenty-six years ago. Until Daisy had insisted on the new chair, Jack had always sat in his father's old wooden spindle back that had once belonged to his mama's dining room set. Though the years, Jack had changed the cushion under his butt, but the chair had always remained the same, only slightly more scratched up and grimy than when his father had run the business.

He punched a few keys on his computer and typed in a freight bill number for a double pump carburetor he needed for a '57 Bel Air. He tracked the part to Tulsa and leaned back into the leather of his new chair. After Tulsa, the carburetor had been shipped to Dallas, then had taken a detour south to Houston. His brows lowered as he turned on the chair massager. He hated to admit it, but Daisy had been right. A lifetime of pulling engines and turning wrenches had taken a toll on him. Now in his mid-forties, he had more aches and pains, and he ate more ibuprofen than his doctor recommended.

The phone beeped and he picked it up. "This is Jack Parrish." He leaned farther back in the chair to take advantage of the rolling massager on his left side. The pain in his back this morning hadn't come from heavy machinery, but from sleeping with his two-year-old daughter wedged between him and Daisy the night before. "What can I do for you?" he asked a kid from Ohio who thought he might have something. Jack listened to him because he liked cars from Ohio. Less humidity. Less rust.

"I've got a 426 Hemi Cuda."

Everything in Jack stilled and he forgot about the pain in his back. A 426 Hemi Cuda was rare as hell.

"Convertible."

He relaxed and laughed. Only twenty-one convertible Hemi Cudas with a 426 had been produced. They were not only rare, they were practically an urban myth. "Check the VIN," he said. A lot of people thought they found something rare when they went through their daddy's and granddaddy's barns and garages, only to check the VINs and discover the engine didn't match the frame. The parts didn't square with the year, and the doors weren't original to rest of the body. Jack's brother, Billy, called them "Frankenstein cars." The brothers bought Frankenstein cars from disappointed sellers all the time and used them for the parts that were original.

"I did check the VIN on the engine and the numbers all match."

"E-mail me some photos." He needed to see proof before he hauled his ass to Ohio to check it out. "I'll call you once I get your pictures." He hung up the phone and shook his head as his son, Nathan, walked into the office, tall and lean and the stamp of Jack's father clear on his forehead. He remembered the first time he'd met Nathan. The first time he'd walked through that office door. A skinny kid with spiky hair, a ring in his bottom lip, and a dog chain around his neck.

He'd held his skateboard beneath one arm, prepared to confront his biological father. The chain, lip ring, and skateboard were gone. His hair was still a bit spiky and he still wore his damn pants too low, but he was a good boy. A good man. He'd always been easygoing and never really given Jack and Daisy a lot of problems growing up. Not even that baby-daddy bullshit with Lindsey a few years back had caused too much heartache. Nathan said he wasn't the daddy, and they believed him. He'd never given them any reason *not* to believe him.

"Got a minute?" Nathan said.

"Sure." His sisters . . . those two little girls were going to make up for it. Eight-year-old Rosemary and two-year-old Lily Belle were sweet-faced tyrants.

Nathan sat in the chair across the desk with something clearly on his mind. He worried his bottom lip before he came out with it. "When did you know that you loved Mom?"

Jack studied his son. When Nathan was serious, his

brows lowered and his eyes turned a darker blue, like now. "You and Holly getting serious?" Jack liked Holly Ann okay. He didn't think she was right for his son, but if Nathan did, he'd have to accept it.

"No."

"No?"

"Holly Ann and I broke up."

"When?"

"Sunday."

It was only Tuesday. Whoever he thought he'd fallen in love with, it had happened pretty quick. Nathan didn't offer anything more and Jack didn't push. His son was a man and he wouldn't pry. Not that he needed to. Daisy could pry anything out of Nathan and then she'd tell him anyway.

"I fell in love with your mama the first time I laid eyes on her. It was the first day of first grade and I saw her standing by herself on playground."

"How did you know you loved her?"

"Well, she had a big red bow in her shiny blond hair, and once I looked into her big brown eyes, I felt my little chest get tight."

Nathan's brows drew together. "What did you do?"

He shrugged. "I told her she had the stupidest hair bow I ever did see. She told me I was stupid, then she burst into tears."

"That wasn't very slick."

He laughed. "I always did have a way with the ladies."

Nate finally smiled as he looked across at him. "Was being with her different?"

"Being? Do you mean sex?"

Nathan nodded.

"Yes." Jack leaned back in his chair. "Being with your mama taught me the difference between sex and making love. Being with her, I learned that making love wasn't just a term interchangeable with sex. Making love is more than just using your dick. It makes you feel things in your heart, whether you want to or not." And God knew, Daisy Lee had always made his chest ache as well as the rest of his body. "You're a Parrish, son. You're like the rest of us. Like me. You're a one-woman man. If you think you've met that woman, you better not let her get away. I caused myself a world of hurt and misery when I let your mama get away."

BECCA CARRIED HER laundry into her apartment and set the basket on her sofa. A week ago, she'd gone to the lake with Nate. And it had taken one week to fall in love and get her heart broken. That was a new record.

She reached for the remote and turned on her television, searching for something to catch her interest enough to keep her from thinking about Nate and the lake. Nate and the barn. Nate and his bed. Nate and his girlfriend.

Just as she settled on a show, a loud knock at the door pulled her attention from *Maury*. She wasn't expecting anyone, and when looked through the peephole, she gazed into a pair of blue eyes gazing back at her.

"Open up. I know you're in there. I saw you carry your laundry inside."

She hugged herself and swung the door open, because the last time he'd seen her she'd been walking from his house, crying her eyes out. This time she wanted him to see that she wasn't crying over him anymore. "What do you want, Nate?"

"I want to start over?"

She shut the door behind him. "With your girlfriend, Holly Ann?"

"Holly Ann isn't my girlfriend."

She folded her arms beneath her breasts. "Since when?"

"Since Sunday. Since the beginning of the summer really. She was just never around so I could break up with her."

"There's always a text."

"That's cold."

"Guys have broken up with me through a dang text message. I got over it."

He nodded. "I probably should have done that, but I didn't think it was necessary until I met you. I thought I'd talk to her when she got back, but then someone unplugged my iPod and gave me a concussion and I was never the same."

"You gave *yourself* a concussion."

He moved toward her and pushed a tendril of hair from her forehead. "I'm sorry, Becca."

"I broke my rules with you, Nate."

"I'm glad."

The backs of her eyes stung despite her hard resolve to show that he couldn't make her cry. "You broke my heart."

"I'll fix it, Becca."

She wasn't so sure she should trust him. No, she was sure. She shouldn't, but she was always willing to listen. "How?"

"I want to start over with you. Start over and do things right." He smiled and reached for her hand. "Instead of getting all annoyed with you because you gave me a concussion, I should have introduced myself." He raised her hand and kissed the backs of her knuckles. "I should have said, 'I'm Nathan Parrish and you're the most beautiful girl I've laid eyes on.'"

That was pretty good. "You're kind of a sweet talker. You've probably said that to other girls."

"Never, but I'm not through. There's more. I'm Nathan Parrish and you're the most beautiful girl I've laid eyes on in my entire life." He slid her hand to the back of his neck. "And at the risk of sounding like that crappy Partridge Family song, I think I love you."

That was really really good. She tried and failed to keep the smile from her lips. "I like that song."

"My daddy told me that Parrish men are susceptible to love at first sight," he continued as if she hadn't interrupted him. "We're one-woman men and when we find our woman, we better never let her go or we'll spend a lot of years kicking ourselves in the ass."

"That sounds serious. And painful."

"If you'd asked me the day before you walked up my driveway in your red shoes, I would have said that I don't believe in that kind of love. But I do now." He dipped his face, and his beautiful blue eyes looked into hers. "And now there's only one thing left to say."

"What?"

"Do you think you love me, Rebecca Ramsey?

Did she love him? "Damn straight." She grinned "Damn straight I do."

Wondering how some of these
characters fell in love?
Find all the couples from *I Do!*
in their own books . . .

Daisy's Back in Town—Daisy and
Jack and their son, Nate
Any Man of Mine—Autumn and Sam
Crazy On You—Lily and Tucker
Rescue Me—Sadie and Vince
Run To You—Stella and Beau

All available now
from Avon Books
and Avon Impulse!

And don't miss the latest novel
from *New York Times* bestselling author
RACHEL GIBSON
featuring Blake and Natalie!

WHAT I LOVE ABOUT YOU

Available now from Avon Books!
Read on for an excerpt . . .

Chapter One

IT'S JUST US. Grab me by the neck and swallow me whole.

Blake Junger wrapped his hands around the thick arms of the Adirondack chair and pushed farther against the back. Desire twisted his stomach, and his muscles hardened. He let out a slow, ragged breath and turned his gaze to the smooth lake. Spiky pine and ponderosa threw jagged shade across his lawn, the wet sandy beach, and the wooden dock floating on the emerald lake. The tops of the trees swayed in an unusually warm October breeze, and the scent of pine forest filled his nose, so strong he could almost taste it. "You're living in God's country now," his realtor had told him when he'd moved into the house in Truly, Idaho, a little over a week ago. The home was four thousand square feet of beautifully crafted wood, its floor-to-ceiling windows reflecting the emerald lake, the deeper green forest, and the brilliant blue sky. It sat on the edge of a small development of homes and had five acres of dense forest on the undeveloped side.

He'd needed a place. A lair. A place to invest a pile of money with good tax benefits. He'd seen this multimillion-dollar property on a Realtor's site, and he'd called and made an offer from his mother's pool deck in Tampa.

He'd trained for high-altitude winter warfare in some of the most frozen and rugged places in the country, one of his favorites being the Idaho Sawtooth mountain range. Blake could live anywhere in the county, but he'd chosen this property on the edge of the wilderness for two reasons: (1) the tax write-offs, and (2) the solitude. The fact that it had a lake in the backyard had sealed the deal.

His parents thought he'd been impulsive. His brother understood. If Truly didn't prove to be an anchor, he would untether and move on.

You want me.

Want and need. Love and hate clogged his chest and dry throat, and he swallowed past the urge to give in. To just say fuck it and give up. He might be living in God's country, but God wasn't paying much attention to Blake Junger these days.

No one will know.

Less than a handful of people even knew where he lived, and he liked it that way. From his time spent on rooftops in Iraq, he'd once lived with a fifty-thousand-dollar bounty placed on his head by Al-Qaeda. Blake was certain the bounty had expired years ago, but even if it hadn't, he wasn't worried about terrorists in Idaho. Hell, a lot of U.S. citizens thought Idaho was in the Midwest next to Iowa anyway. He was much more worried that his well-intentioned family would pop up and camp out in his living room. Watching to make sure he didn't fuck up and end up on his face somewhere.

I'll warm you up. Make you feel good.

Blake returned his gaze to a bottle sitting on the wood cable spool a few feet from his left foot. Sunlight touched the neck and shone through the amber liquid inside. Johnnie Walker. His best friend. The constant that never changed. The one thing in the world he could count on. The hot splash in his mouth. The kick and punch to his throat and stomach. The warmth spreading across his flesh and the buzz in his head. He loved it. Loved it more than friends and family. More than his job and latest mission. More than women and sex. He'd given up a lot for Johnnie. Then Johnnie had gone and turned on him. Johnnie was a big lie.

I'm not the enemy.

Blake had faced enemies before. In Iraq, Afghanistan, Africa, and too many shithole countries to count. He'd faced and conquered those enemies. He had a footlocker full of medals and commendations. He'd been shot twice, had screws in his knee, and had fractured his feet and ankles more times than he could recall. He'd served his country without regret or remorse. When he retired from the battlefield, he thought he'd left the enemy behind. Thought he was done fighting, but he was wrong. This enemy was deeper and darker than any he had faced before.

You can stop after one drink.

It whispered lies and plagued his waking hours. It lived in his soul. It had a bounty on his life. A bounty he couldn't ignore. There was no getting away from it. No leave. No passes. No stand-down time. No hiding in the dark as it passed him by. No dialing in his scope to take it out. Like the enemies he'd faced on the battlefield, if he did not defeat it, he would die. No doubt about it, but the problem was, he craved the taste of this particular death in his mouth.

You don't have a problem.

Out of all the things that had been hammered into his head at the fancy rehab his brother had forced him into, one of the things he did believe was that if he did not stop, he would lose his life. He'd been through too much to be taken out by a bottle of Johnnie. Too much to let his addiction win.

The craving rolled through him and he set his jaw against it. His addiction doctors and counselors had preached avoidance, but that wasn't Blake's way. He didn't avoid demons. He faced them head-on. He didn't need a twelve-step program or daily meetings. He was not powerless over his addiction. He was Special Warfare Operator First Class Blake Junger. Retired from SEAL Team Six, and one of the deadliest snipers in the history of warfare. That wasn't a brag, just a fact. To admit he was powerless would be admitting defeat. There was no quit, no giving up. Those words were not in a Junger's vocabulary. Not in his or his twin brother, Beau's. They'd been raised to win. To push themselves and each other. To be the best at everything. To follow in the famous footsteps of their father, Captain William T. Junger, a legend in the SEAL teams. The old man had earned a tough reputation in Vietnam and Grenada and countless other clandestine engagements. He was a tough warrior, loyal to the teams and his country, and he expected his sons to follow. Blake had done what had been expected of him while Beau had signed with the Marine Corps just to spite the old man.

At the time, Blake had been pissed at his brother. All their lives they'd talked about serving in the teams together, but Beau had stormed off and joined the jarheads. In hindsight, it was a blessing that they'd served in different branches.

They were monozygotic twins, had split from the same egg, and were so alike they could pass one for the other. They were not different sides of the same coin. They were identical sides, and it was no surprise that each had signed up for sniper school in their respective branches. No surprise that each earned a reputation for his accuracy and lethal shots, but when it came to numbers, Blake had more confirmed kills.

The brothers had always been competitive. Their mother claimed that even in the womb they'd fought each other for more room. At the age of five, Beau had been the faster swimmer, had won blue ribbons while Blake had won red. Second place spurred Blake on to work harder, and the next year the two traded places on the winner's podium. In high school, if Blake won more wrestling matches one season, his brother worked to win more the next, and because they were identical twins, people compared the two in more than looks. Beau was the smart one. Blake was the strong one. Beau ran faster. Blake was the charming one. A day later, the script would flip and Blake would be smarter and faster. But no matter how many times the comparisons spun in opposite directions, Blake had always been the more charming twin. Even Beau conceded that win.

If they'd both been SEALs, people would have just naturally compared their service. They would have compared numbers and missions and ranks. While the brothers were extremely proud of their service, and the American lives they'd saved with their deadly shots, a man's death, even that of an insurgent hell-bent on killing Americans, just wasn't something they felt the need to compete over. Neither had crouched in the shadows of a shithole hut or rocky crag, alternately sweating like whores in church or freezing his nuts off, thinking he needed to compete. Both knew that numbers were more a matter of opportunity than skill, although neither would ever confess that out loud.

Since Beau's retirement from the Marines, he'd started a personal security company. Beau was the successful one. The settled one. The one getting married. Beau was the one who'd used his skills to create opportunity for fellow retired military personnel.

And Blake was the drunk. Since his retirement from the Navy a year ago, he was the one who'd used his skills to make money as a hired gun. He worked for a private military security firm, and he was the one who'd hopped from hot spot to hostage situation. From country to open seas, living a seemly unsettled life.

And Blake was the one who'd needed rehab to face his biggest demon. Like all enemies, he'd faced it head-on, only to discover that the consequence of sobriety was that at any moment, a flash or smell or sound could spin his clear and sober head around. That a flash in sunlight, or the smell of dust and sweat, or a high-pitched whistle could crawl up his spine and stop him in his tracks. Could make him drop and look for something that wasn't there. The flashbacks didn't happen often and didn't last more than a few seconds, but they always left him disoriented and edgy. Angry at his loss of control.

He looked at the bottle of Johnnie. At the blue and gold label and sun filtering through the rare scotch whisky. He'd paid three hundred dollars for the bottle of booze, and he craved it in the pit of his stomach. It tugged and pulled at his insides, and the sharp edge of need cut across his skin.

One drink. Calm the craving. Dull the sharp edges.

Blake's knuckle popped as he tightened his grasp on the chair.

Just one more. You can stop tomorrow.

The craving grew stronger, pinching his skull. Wasn't day sixty-two supposed to be easier than day one? His stomach rolled and his ears buzzed in his head. He picked up the camera by his hip and stood. He wrapped the black and yellow strap around his forearm and pointed his Nikon SLR at Johnnie. Six months ago, he'd stared down the scope of a bolt-action TAC–338 in Mexico City with two corrupt Mexican police officers sharing his crosshairs. These days, he shot his enemy with a camera. He looked through the viewfinder and dialed up the bottle. His hands shook and he tightened his grasp.

"What are you doing?"

Blake spun around and almost dropped the camera. "Holy fuck!" A little girl in a pink shirt and long blond ponytail stood behind his chair. "Where in the hell did you come from?" He'd lost his touch if a little kid could sneak up on him.

With her thumb she pointed next door. "You said two bad words."

He scrubbed his face with one hand and lowered the camera by the strap to his chair. She'd scared the shit out of him, and that wasn't easy to do. "And you're trespassing."

She scrunched up her nose. "What's that mean?"

He'd never been around kids and couldn't even guess her age. She was about as tall as his navel and had big blue eyes. "Trespass?"

"Yeah."

"It means you're in my yard."

"I know it's your yard." She actually rolled those blue eyes at him. "I saw you move in."

A five-foot stretch of pine and underbrush separated the two properties, and he glanced at the neighboring yard through the trees. The woman living there was working in the flower garden that she had managed to scratch out of the forest. Ass-up in pink and purple flowers, her shorts rode up just high enough to show the naked curve of her butt. He'd noticed her before today. He might be a drunk, white-knuckling sixty-two days' sobriety, but he was still a man. A man who appreciated a nice ass pointed his way. He'd never seen the woman's face. Just the back of her blond head and her sweet butt cheeks.

"What's your name?"

He turned his attention back toward the child and wondered if he should feel guilty for having sexual thoughts about the kid's mama. "Blake." He didn't feel guilty. He just wondered if he *should* feel guilty. "Is that your mom?"

"Yeah. She's not at the store today."

He couldn't recall hearing a man's voice coming from next door as he'd studied the mom's butt. "Where's your dad?"

"He doesn't live with us." She swung her arms from side to side. "I don't like bees."

He frowned down at the little squid in front of him. He didn't know what bees had to do with anything, but after sixty-two days, nausea rolled through him like it was the first. He felt like he might puke and dropped his shaking hands to his hips.

"You're weally weally big."

He was a little over six foot and weighed two-twenty. In the past few months he'd dropped twenty pounds. One of the last times he'd seen his twin, his brother had called Blake "a pudgy fucker." They'd been slugging it out at the time. Arguing over who was the better shot and the toughest superhero, Batman or Superman. Beau had been wrong about Superman but right about the fat. After Blake had retired from the teams, he'd had time to kill between security jobs. He'd stopped working out as much and started drinking more. "How old are you, kid?"

"Five." Her arms fell to her side and she tossed her head. "I'm not a kid."

Behind him Johnnie whispered, *I'm still here. Waiting.* Blake ignored the whisper. He needed to jog or swim. He needed to wear himself out, but that didn't mean he'd quit and let Johnnie win. No, a warrior knew when to withdraw and come back hard.

"I'm a hoss."

Blake moved his head from side to side as the pain in his skull thumped his brain. "What the hell's a hoss?"

She rolled her eyes again like he was a bit slow. "A hh-hooooosssss."

Blake spoke perfect English, broken Arabic, and fluent split-fucking-infinitive. He'd never heard of a hoss.

"My name is Bow Tie."

"Bow Tie?" What the hell kind of name was that?

"I have yellow hair with white spots." She tossed her head again and stomped one foot. "I have a white mane and tail. I'm fancy."

"Are you saying 'horse'?" Jesus. She was turning the ache in his head to a stabbing pain. "You're a horse?"

"Yes, and I'm weally fast. Do you want to see me race?"

He'd never been around kids. He didn't even know if he liked kids. He was fairly sure he didn't like this kid. She thought she was a "hoss," couldn't say some of her R's, and looked at him like *he* was slow in the head. "Negative. You should go home now."

"No. I can stay."

"You've been here long enough now. Your mother is probably wondering where you are."

"My mom won't mind." She stomped the ground with one sandaled foot, then took off. She ran in a big circle around Blake. She actually galloped around and around. And God help him, with her head bobbing and her ponytail flying behind her, she kind of resembled a little pony.

Around and around she ran, stopping a few times to paw at the air and neigh. "Hey kid," he called to her, but she just tossed her head and kept going. The pull of Johnnie rode him hard and irritation broke out across his skin. He had better things to do than stand there as a weird little girl acted like a horse. Better things, like go for a jog or swim or poke himself in the eye with a stick. "Time to go home." She pretended not to hear him. What did she call herself? "Stop, Bow Tie!"

"Say whoa, girl," she managed between rapid breaths.

He didn't take orders from children. He was an adult. He wanted to tear out his hair. Christ almighty. "Shit."

Around she ran, her pale cheeks turning pink. "That was a bad word."

Blake frowned. "Whoa, girl."

She finally stopped directly in front of him and blew out a breath. "I went weally fast."

"You need to run home."

"That's okay. I can play for . . ." She paused before adding, "Five moe minutes."

He'd lived in a dirt hole and crawled through swamps. He'd eaten bugs and pissed in Gatorade bottles. For twenty years, his life had consisted of hard, rough edges. When he'd retired from the teams, he'd had to make a deliberate effort to keep the F-word out of every sentence and his hand off his nuts. He'd had to remember that in civilian life, creative swearing wasn't a competitive sport and that ball scratching wasn't a public event. He had to remember the manners his mother had pounded into his and Beau's heads. Nice, polite behavior toward everyone from little kids to little old ladies. Today he wanted this kid gone before he ripped his skin off, and he chose not to remember those nice manners. He purposely narrowed his eyes and gave the kid the hard steel gaze that he'd used to make terrorists cower.

"What's wrong with your eyes?"

She didn't seem at all afraid. She was definitely a little slow in the head. Another time he might have taken that into consideration. "Get your ass in your own yard."

She gasped. "You said a bad word."

"Go home, little girl."

She pointed at the cat on the front of her T-shirt. "I'm a big girl!"

Another day, another time, he might have admired the kid's guts. He leaned forward and towered over her like his father used to do to him and Beau. "I *shit* bigger than you," he said, just like his old man.

The kid sucked in a scandalized breath but wasn't intimidated at all. She wasn't shaking in her little shoes. Was there something wrong with the kid, besides her thinking she was a horse, or was he losing his touch?

"Charlotte?"

Blake and the kid spun toward the sound of a woman's voice. She stood a few feet away, wearing a little yellow T-shirt and those shorts he'd had the privilege of seeing from behind. The shadow of a big straw hat hid her face and rested just above the bow of her full lips. Pretty mouth, nice legs, great ass. Probably something wrong with her eyes.

"Mama!" The kid ran to her mother and threw herself on the woman's waist.

"You know you aren't supposed to leave the yard, Charlotte Elizabeth." The shade of her hat slid down her throat and T-shirt to her breasts as she looked down at her child. "You're in big trouble."

Nice-size breasts, smooth curve in her waist. Yeah, probably had funky eyes.

"That man is weally mean," the kid wailed. "He said bad words at me."

The sudden sobbing was so suspect he might have laughed if he was in a laughing mood. Behind him, Johnnie whispered his name, and in front, the shade of a straw hat rested on the top of a nice pair of breasts. The shadow dipped into her smooth cleavage, and lust plunged straight down Blake's pants. He went from irritation to desire to a combination of both in the blink of an eye.

The brim of the hat rose to the bow of her lip again. "I heard him." The corners of her mouth dipped in a disapproving frown.

His frown matched hers. He'd always avoided women like her. Women with children. Women with children were looking for daddies, and he'd never wanted kids. His or anyone else's.

"Please don't swear at my child."

"Please keep your child out of my yard." Women with children wanted men who wanted relationships. He wasn't a relationship kind of guy. Out of all the SEAL teams, Team Six had the highest divorce rate for a reason. It was filled with men who loved to throw themselves out of airplanes and get shot out of torpedo tubes. Filled with good men who weren't any good at relationships. Men like him, and until recently, like his brother. Men like his father, whose wives divorced them after twenty years of serial cheating.

"Fine." Her lips pursed like she was going to hit him or kiss him. Off the top of his head, he'd guess the former. "But what kind of man talks like that to a child?"

The kind who was white-knuckling his sixty-second

day of sobriety. The kind who wanted to pour some Johnnie down his throat, say fuck it, and dive face-first into
soft cleavage. "What kind of mother lets her child roam
around unsupervised?"

She gasped. "She was supervised."

"Uh-huh." He'd made her mad. Good. Now maybe she'd
leave. Leave him to his fight with Johnnie and himself.

"Charlotte knows better than to leave our yard."

He pointed out the obvious. "This isn't your yard."

"She's never run off before."

He couldn't see her eyes, but he could feel her angry
gaze. All hot and fiery. He liked hot and fiery. He liked
it riding him like a banshee. Wild, screaming his name,
and . . . Christ. His lust for Johnnie and this nameless
woman made him dizzy. "Only takes once for her to get
hit by a truck," he heard himself say between clenched
teeth. "I had a dog that only got out once. Bucky ended
up as axle grease for a Chevy Silverado." He shook his
head. God, he'd loved that poodle. "He'd been a damn
good dog, too."

Her pink mouth opened and closed like she was
speechless. Then she waved a hand at the bottle of Johnnie and obviously found her voice. "Are you drunk?"

"No. Haven't had a drop." He wished he could blame
his erection on Johnnie.

"Then you don't have an excuse. You're just a . . . a . . ."
She paused to cover the girl's ears with her palms. "A
raging asshole."

She'd get no argument from him.

"I heard that," the kid said into her mother's stomach.

"Come on, Charlotte." She grabbed the kid's hand and stormed off. He could practically see the steam shooting out of her ears.

So much for being the charming twin.

He shrugged, and his gaze fell to her nice butt.

Fuck it. Charming was for nice guys, and he hadn't felt nice for a very long time.

About the Author

New York Times bestselling author **RACHEL GIBSON** began her fiction career at age sixteen, when she ran her car into the side of a hill, retrieved the bumper, and drove to a parking lot, where she strategically scattered the car's broken glass all about. She told her parents she'd been the victim of a hit-and-run and they believed her. She's been making up stories ever since, although she gets paid better for them nowadays.

Discover great authors, exclusive offers, and more at hc.com.